Fledgling

LUCY HOPE

nosy
crow

For Kev
My rock

First published in the UK in 2021 by Nosy Crow Ltd
The Crow's Nest, 14 Baden Place
Crosby Row, London SE1 1YW

Nosy Crow and associated logos are trademarks and/or registered
trademarks of Nosy Crow Ltd

ISBN: 978 1 83994 188 7

A CIP catalogue record for this book is available from
the British Library.

Printed and bound in the UK by Clays Ltd, Elcograf S.p.A

Typeset by Tiger Media

Pape... wood grown in
sustainable forests

Chapter One

Edenburg, Bavaria. 1900

Our house perches on top of a tall rock. My great-great-grandfather, Walter Engel, built it years ago, hauling the foundation stones up by rope and pulley. It was a simple place at the beginning – just a hotchpotch of rooms looking down on the Bratvian Forest and the small town of Edenburg. With a growing collection of stuffed owls, Walter built another storey dedicated to their display, and an annex to the side for his book collection. In his middle years he built two more floors for his frequent house guests. When Mother inherited the house, she added a music room at the top. Today our house stretches precariously to the sky, a monument to the dreams of five generations of the Engel family.

Living on a rock presented various challenges over the years, particularly the problem of how to reach the house without crampons and climbing boots. My great-grandfather designed a mechanical winch system that bounced white-knuckled visitors up and down the rock at great speed. My grandfather's somewhat safer solution was to use explosives to blast out a road that encircled the rock like a helter-skelter. And to this day that is how we come and go from our eyrie, either on foot or by carriage.

So that is where we live. Mother, Papa, Grandma and me. At night I can see München, miles away, where Mother performs at the opera house. When not on stage, she spends her days in the music room rehearsing for her next performance.

Grandma moved back in with us when the illness took hold last year. It's spreading through her body now, gnawing at her bones. She used to look after me when Mother was performing and I was too young to leave alone. We'd play games like I spy or hide-and-seek among the owls. When I was six she taught me the Bavarian dances of her childhood: the Zweifacher and the Schuhplattler.

I sit with her now, holding her hand, squeezing cool water on to her parched lips with a small sponge. She's a remnant of her former self. A heap of hollow bones, sunken cheeks and white hair.

Remembering the nurses are coming later to see her, I check the dials on the brass morphine pump. It was designed by Grandpa years ago to relieve my uncle Killian's pain after he returned from the war with a shattered leg. The bellows hiss and heave noisily and I wonder how she sleeps through the racket. I adjust the settings, allowing a little more of the powerful medicine to flow into her veins.

I gently kiss her hand and head back to my room.

★

A storm is brewing. Living high like this, we see the weather coming before anyone else.

Storm's coming, I tap into my little Morse code machine, warning Raphael, my one and only friend in Edenburg. People tend to stay away from us these days, what with the house, and the owls … and Mother.

Thanks, he taps back.

I glance down at his house at the edge of town and

see him lean out of his room to pull his window closed.

Mother is in her music room, as always. I know she'll keep *her* windows open, despite the storm. People whisper when they see her, standing at a window, as if performing to the heavens. She's singing *"Agnus Dei"* – Lamb of God. The wind catches her voice and it weaves round our rock and up into the eye of the approaching storm.

The world becomes dark. Rain pelts at my window. Mother sings. Grandma's pump sighs.

I hear a tap at my window and press my face against the rain-soaked glass but see nothing. I throw myself back on to my bed and return to my book. I hear the tapping again. I try to ignore it, but it comes again. Curiosity finally overwhelms me, and I pad back to the window, planning to open it just an inch. The wind catches it, throwing it open and the storm fills my room. Something whistles past my ear and lands with a gentle thud on the bed. I slam my window closed, my hands shaking. Turning back to my bed I see what looks like a bird of prey lying in a sodden, trembling heap on my eiderdown.

I pick it up carefully, wrap it in a shawl and hold it on my lap like a baby. Having grown up with the collection of stuffed owls, I should be able to identify it.

Eventually the creature's trembling subsides, and I unwrap my little package to see what's inside, certain it's just a barn owl.

I examine it, gently lifting its wings, turning it over. My heart stops. It can't be. I tap a message to Raphael again.

Please come. I need you.

Now?

Yes, I reply. *Now.*

The creature seems to be in a deep sleep. I barely dare touch it, terrified it might wake. I have never seen anything like it, but I'm certain I know what it is. Four tiny wings protrude from its shoulder blades. Its body is covered in scruffy feathers. The skin on its hands and feet has the feel of parchment. I touch the sparse soft hair on its head. It is dark, like mine, but finer. Still wet from the storm, it begins to shiver. I wrap the shawl round it again. Its pale face with tightly shut eyes is that of a sleeping infant.

★

Raphael comes before the storm has passed. He's drenched.

"I have something to show you," I say.

He bends down to kiss my cheek. "Hello, Cassie, how are you? How lovely to see you!"

"Oh, sorry. Hello, Raphael. But something strange has happened and I don't know what to do."

He looks down at me, and then at the bundle in my arms.

"I think you need to sit down," I say, touching the bed next to me.

I cannot think of anyone else in the world I can trust with this. Gentle Raphael is the obvious and only choice. He sits and I place the creature on his knee. He unwraps the shawl a little.

He looks at me. "Is this what I think it is?"

I nod. He wraps it up again, his eyes wide. "Where on earth did you find her?"

"She was blown into my room in the storm. I heard a tapping at the window. I opened it and she landed on my bed, just here." I point to the patch on the bed, which is still wet. "I thought you only found them in the Bible," I add. "I didn't think they actually existed. And I thought they were supposed to be boys."

"Those stories are from a different time," he says quietly.

"Do you think she's some kind of angel?"

"I think she might be a cherub, actually," he says. "They're quite different to angels."

I remember the exhibition of religious paintings

Grandma took me to see in the Glaspalast nearly two years ago. The main hall was filled with oil paintings and statues of cherubs – but they were pink, well-fed infants with little wings that couldn't possibly have lifted them into the air. They were nothing like this strange creature.

"What do you think I should do with her?" I whisper.

"I don't know," he says, handing her back to me. "It's not something I know much about." He turns away as if to avoid my gaze.

"We could look in the library. See if there's anything there on cherubs…" I say, visualising the shelves in the old library downstairs. "There's a section on feathered creatures, and definitely some religious books."

He nods. "But we need to be careful. It's possible someone, or *something*, will be out looking for her."

My heart misses a beat. "What sort of *something*?"

"I'm not sure." He walks to the window and looks up at the sky, frowning.

The storm is subsiding but dark clouds still swirl around the house, accentuating the gloom in my room.

"Do you think we should feed her?" I say, shivering.

"I don't think so," he says. "I suspect she needs something other than food to stay alive."

"Such as?"

He shakes his head. "I just think her needs will be

quite different to those of a human baby." He hesitates. "And I don't think you should tell your parents about her for now."

I nod. "Where could she have come from?"

He looks at me, as if considering something. "Perhaps she lost the others in this storm. Like a bird separated from its flock."

I look at him. "The other *whats*?" I say, the hairs on the back of my neck pricking. "You think there are more out there like her?" I glance out of the window nervously.

"Probably not many like her. Most likely angels." He turns from the window to face me. "Was your—" He stops himself.

"Was my what?"

"Oh, nothing."

"What is it, Raphael?"

"Your mother was singing earlier, wasn't she?" he says, after a pause.

"Yes, of course she was. She's always singing. What are you saying?"

"Well, I know it sounds peculiar, but I think angels might communicate by song. Like whales. I'm wondering if she was drawn to your mother's voice. Maybe she thought her singing was the host calling to her."

"By *host*, you mean other angels?" I say, even though

I know the answer.

He nods.

"And you think they'll come looking for their baby?"

"Possibly. I don't know, Cassie. I don't know much more than you! But I do know she isn't a baby. She's probably thousands of years old."

I glance down at the creature in my arms, at her strange paper-like skin and delicate feathers. I cannot believe she is so ancient.

Chapter Two

We climb the narrow staircase to the owlery, the room that leads through to the library. I hug the cherub close. Her heart seems to beat in time with mine.

The owlery hasn't changed since my great-great-grandfather established his collection of stuffed owls here nearly a hundred years ago. Wide-eyed creatures stare at us from ebony-framed display cases as we pass. My favourite, Otto, a pygmy owl, sits caged for eternity with his friend Fritz, the tawny owl. Eric, the giant eagle owl, stands majestically in the middle of the room in a vast dome-shaped glass case, his wings outstretched, his eyes wild. Tiny handwritten labels hang from the owls' claws, identifying each of the thirty-eight creatures by their Latin names.

The owls are my responsibility, and I have established a daily routine of dusting feathers, replacing rusting pins, and polishing cases until they gleam. Grandma named me as official curator when it became clear to everyone that Mother would not keep the owls safe. This responsibility has been mine since my tenth birthday.

The ancient heating system clatters and crashes as we tread on creaking floorboards. I kick the cast-iron pipe that runs along the side of the room and the noise subsides. I'm pleased to be wearing my sturdy boots.

We pass through the door at the far end and step into the library. It is even darker here than in the owlery as the room was designed with just one small window to protect the books from the effects of sunlight. Raphael reaches across the battered leather desk in the centre of the room and flicks the switch on the desk lamp. I breathe in the familiar smell of ancient tobacco mingled with old books and leather, a sensory legacy from a great-great-grandfather I never knew.

The walls are lined from floor to ceiling with books of all shapes and sizes, with subjects ranging from philosophy to anatomy and dancing cats. Of course there is a whole section on birds, identified by a handmade ALL THINGS FEATHERED sign. I hope to find something useful here, but then I wonder if texts on cherubs would be hidden somewhere else. Might they be within the section on ALL THINGS SUPERNATURAL, or even in WORLD RELIGIONS?

"Where should we start looking?" asks Raphael, glancing about the room.

"I guess somewhere around here," I say, running my fingers along the spine of a tall leather-bound book entitled *Owl Taxidermy for Novices* within the "feathered" section. Walter Engel organised his library in such a way that makes it almost impossible to find what you are looking for, but I have a distinct feeling he might have placed books on angels close to the reference books on owls.

I hear Mother calling and my heart sinks. She doesn't call me in the usual way a mother might. Instead she sings my name in the character of her latest role. This month she has been rehearsing to play Malwina in the opera *Der Vampyr*.

"Cassie! Cassie! Cassie! Cassie!" she sings, in a rising arpeggio, increasing in volume with each note. "Cassie!

Cassie! Cassie! Cassie!"

I put my head down, hoping she might forget about me. But she doesn't stop, and her voice rises steadily until I can no longer bear it.

"Would you like me to come with you?" asks Raphael.

I want more than anything for Raphael to come with me, but it's best if I'm on my own. It's the unpredictability that's the problem; I never know how she might be from one moment to the next these days.

"I think you should stay here," I say, holding the creature tightly in my arms. I don't want to let her go; with her heart pounding next to mine, she is beginning to feel like part of me. "And you need to look after the cherub while I'm gone." I hand her to him. "I'm worried about what Bram will do if he sees her." He's as gentle as a kitten with me, but brutal with anything feathered. "He brought down a sparrowhawk on the rock just yesterday."

Raphael smiles. "If you're sure, but call if you need me."

I leave Raphael in the library and head towards the spiral staircase that leads up to Mother's music room.

Chapter Three

I knock before I open the door and step inside. Mother is standing with her back to me, surveying the storm through one of the small leaded windows. The room seems darker than usual. She is dressed as if about to walk on stage, in a long silver gown that falls to her ankles and a voluminous cape. Hearing me enter, she turns to face me. In the lamplight she is as white as snow. Her lips are red as blood.

"Ah, Cassie darling," she says. "Where have you been? I am quite hoarse from calling you."

"I was busy," I reply, probably too stiffly.

"Oh, you're always busy with something, Cassie."

I say nothing and stare at my feet. She is right, of course. I am always busy: with the owls, the plumbing, ensuring Emaline the maid knows what Mother has requested for dinner, checking Papa is safe.

"Is the boy here?" she asks, her eyes searching me. In this light they are the green of the verdigris roof over the music room.

"Which boy?" I say, even though I know exactly who she's talking about.

"Oh, you know, the boy from the town."

I look up at her. Should I deny he's here?

"Oh, don't play the innocent with me, Cassie. I've heard the two of you crashing about downstairs."

"His name is Raphael, Mother. And he's my friend."

The remains of a crystal glass lie in smithereens at the base of the music stand. I pick up a page of sheet music from the chiffonier, kneel down and scoop up as many fragments as I can without cutting my fingers.

"Leave that, Cassie. Emaline will deal with it later."

Emaline is old, and I hate seeing her bending to clear up after one of Mother's rages. She used to haul herself up our rock every morning in the rusting winch system. Now, with the arthritis gnawing at her knuckles and toes, she shuffles up our helter-skelter road every day before it gets light – like an old snail – to look after us. I think she has enough to do without clearing up broken glass. I sweep up the tiny shards as well as I can, worried that Papa might tread on them when he returns from München. He's recently taken to walking about the house in bare feet, oblivious to the freezing floorboards. I wonder for a moment if the glass had been flung at him.

Mother sinks into the chaise longue and sweeps a pale hand across her forehead, sighing. She's still beautiful, of course. Her ink-black hair, now streaked with grey, rises up from her head in a mass of shining spirals. Grandpa used to laugh, when I was little, about how "his girls" had hair like our helter-skelter road. People comment that I look just like Mother. But my hair seems to have even more energy than hers. Every morning I tug at it, rubbing in Papa's Macassar oil in an effort to bring it under control.

"Get me a drink, darling," Mother says, "my vocal cords are fatigued." She lifts her chin, closes her eyes and "ahhhs". "Snap-snap, Cassie," she says, her eyes still closed, clicking her fingers.

I pick up a bottle of schnapps and sniff its contents, furious with myself for not telling her to pour her own drink. She's always summoning me from some distant room in the house to pour a drink or run an errand. But I don't want to argue with her today. I have more important things to do.

I choose a glass that looks cleaner than the others, pour some of the clear liquid into it and pass it to her.

"Are you likely to change your dress some time this month, darling?" she asks brightly, looking me up and down.

I smooth my dress with my hands. It's plain black – and practical – and much easier to hoist out of the way when climbing the rock or carrying out maintenance around the house than a full-length dress. She's staring at my legs now, and I tuck one foot behind the other, trying to somehow make myself less visible. I have a hole in my stocking. I hope she hasn't noticed.

"So – the boy," she says.

I do not want to discuss Raphael with her.

"What is it his father does for a living? Remind me, darling. I can't quite remember."

"You know what his father does, Mother. He's a cobbler. He repairs your shoes."

"Ah, yes," she tinkles. "I had completely forgotten.

How sweet. Rather like someone out of a fairy tale!"

She sips her schnapps without leaving a trace of lipstick on the glass.

"You're looking so pale, darling. Let me apply a little rouge."

I step backwards. "No thank you, Mother, I have things to do. Can I go now?"

"Oh, well, of course, if you'd rather spend time with the *cobbler's son*, than with your own mother—" She takes another slug of the schnapps.

I head towards the door, hoping our meeting is over. I'm desperate to get back to the cherub. And to Raphael.

"Oh, and one other thing—"

My heart sinks. What now?

"I want you to get rid of the owls."

My hand is on the doorknob. I grip it hard and take a deep breath before turning to face her.

"I am not getting rid of the owls," I say, my heart suddenly thudding. What would she expect me to do with them? Sell them? Throw them down the rock? She knows how important they are to me. The owls are better listeners than Mother will ever be, and they don't criticise the state of my stockings. And then there was Grandpa's dying instruction that they should be preserved at all costs. He was quite insistent. "Whatever happens to the family," he'd said, "anything can be sold off – but not the owls. Promise me that, Cassie." Of course I promised. I didn't ask him why this was so important to him because he died shortly afterwards. But I kept my promise, and now they're a part of me – a part of my daily life. I don't think I could ever "get rid" of them.

"If you don't, darling, then I will. And they'll end up somewhere much nicer if you deal with them." The schnapps is already taking effect, making her voice drawl slightly.

"You know I can't," I hiss, trying to control the panic in my voice.

"I'm afraid you're going to have to, Cassie," she says, rising from the chaise longue. She's almost a head taller than me. "Your father is taking up too much space in here." She gestures towards a small pile of boxes under one of the windows. "I can't bear it any longer. The owlery will be his room, where he can spread his things about willy-nilly for all I care. It's *my* house remember, Cassie."

"I can't do it," I say. "And Grandma won't allow it either. You know that." I stand, feeling not tall enough, and face her.

"Well, Grandma's hardly going to argue, is she, what with that ghastly contraption huffing and puffing day and night. I suspect the owls are at the bottom of her list of priorities just now."

"I won't do it!" I mutter as I stomp out of the room, forgetting Mother has the hearing of a bat.

"Oh yes you will, Cassie!" she shouts after me.

Chapter Four

I'm still shaking when I find Raphael in the library. He's bathed in the light of the old desk lamp, absorbed in an enormous book, the cherub nestled, still asleep, in his arms.

As I creep in behind him, the old floorboards shift noisily under my boots. It's impossible to walk quietly anywhere in this house.

He turns to face me and smiles. "How did it go?"

"She wants me to dispose of the owls," I say. I don't mention what she said about him.

"Your grandma would never allow it. Your mother knows that."

The creak of Grandma's pump weaves its way from the floor above. I know she can no longer help me.

"She wants Papa out of the music room. Apparently he's taking up too much space." I almost laugh at the thought, as Papa doesn't take up much space at all. Big-hearted, but damaged, like his friend, my uncle Killian, who died years ago, he shuffles about the house most days humming into his giant pipe-stained beard or squirrelled away in his workshop. Grandpa once explained that "his soul was shattered, after what happened in the war". He told me there was no contraption that could repair that.

"She'll probably change her mind," says Raphael. "Why don't you wait and see what happens? It might just be one of her whims."

I nod and pull up a chair next to him.

"Has she been like this all the time I've been away?" I ask, looking down at the cherub, wishing more than anything to take her back.

"Yes, she hasn't moved. I'm wondering if she might be traumatised, and this deep sleep is some sort of protective mechanism."

Fledgling

As if he's read my mind, he gently passes her back to me. I hold her tightly and feel a comforting warmth spread through my body again. Within seconds our hearts are beating in the same rhythm, like earlier. I didn't think I'd imagined it.

The book Raphael has open on the desk looks ancient. "It's a codex," he whispers, "an illuminated manuscript, handwritten on vellum. I think it's very old."

I touch the hand-cut edges of the book, being careful not to get my fingers near the illustrations. Noticing my nails are black I pull my hands away and tuck them round the sleeping cherub instead. The drawings are the brightest gold, despite their age, and the elaborate borders are laced with interlinked miniature cherubs. I'm worried for a moment it might be written in Latin and am relieved to see it is in the Old Bavarian language.

"Where did you find it?" I say. I am certain I have never seen it before. Whenever I went to visit Grandpa in the library as a child, he'd pull out old books for us to look through together. He'd explain how vellum was made from calfskin and that it lasted for hundreds or even thousands of years. I loved listening to his stories of how early craftsmen stretched and scraped the material and whitened it with chalk until it was ready to be written on by scribes with goose-feather quills. Sometimes we

23

even made our own quills when one of the owls dropped a feather or we found an eagle feather in the forest. We mixed up solutions of oak apples, lampblack and black iron salts for ink, and wrote stories together. I remember laughing when he told me how people used stale urine or earwax to improve the texture of the gold paint for the illuminated texts.

"It was with the religious books," says Raphael, nodding towards one of the bookshelves. "It looks like it hasn't been opened for a long time. There's no title on the spine, or anywhere on the cover, which is why it wasn't obvious."

I lean in closer still, and my arm brushes against his. He's generating as much heat as the cherub. He turns to me and smiles briefly before returning to the text.

The book is thick, probably a hundred or more pages, and huge, taking up most of the desk. The leather cover is a faded red. It is coated in dust, and as I run my fingers over the pages, tiny particles jump about us. I wonder briefly if it is the dust of my ancestors – skin fragments from another age.

We sit side by side and read together. I listen to the sounds of the house, worrying Mother might pounce on us unexpectedly – but I've never seen her in the library, and with the door closed I feel safe.

I can read Old Bavarian, but I'm slow to make sense of the elaborate lettering. As I pick my way through the heavy script, reading out loud, I catch my breath.

"*Cherubs are the highest in the hierarchy of angels, sent to Earth for only the most crucial missions.*"

I gasp. "Do you think she's here on a mission? What could she possibly be here for?"

Raphael shakes his head, but says nothing.

"*Any person who causes harm to a cherub will face the fury of the host.*"

Fury of the host? What does that mean? I glance at Raphael, but his face is unreadable.

Further down the page we find detailed physical descriptions of cherubs, and even a little sketch with annotations. According to what is written here, cherubs vary significantly in appearance, and are often nothing like those in the traditional religious drawings seen in churches and bibles. The cherubs drawn and described here *are* baby-like, but their bodies are feathered and four small wings protrude from their shoulder blades. Some are so pale they are almost transparent, yet others have dark skin and black feathers. The cherub in my arms has skin the colour of alabaster and feathers in shades of beige and umber.

Raphael and I look at each other and then down at

the cherub.

"*A cherub on Earth draws sustenance from the chosen host, for love is the food that nurtures them.*"

"What do you think that means?" I say. "Does it mean the host of angels? How can they draw sustenance from them if they are elsewhere?"

Raphael shakes his head. "Perhaps it's a different type of host they're talking about."

In the margin, overlapping the illustrations, is a mess of faded scribbled notes, a later addition to the more formal writing elsewhere on the page. The word *predator* appears several times. Towards the top of the page the same word has been underlined many times in the firm, scratchy sweep of someone's quill. Whoever wrote this did so in a hurry. There are mistakes and crossings out, and the ink has smudged as if the author slammed the book shut before the ink had been given time to dry.

There is a sketch of a giant birdlike creature in the top right corner of the page. In another sketch in the wide bottom margin is what looks like a thunder cloud. It is anvil-shaped – and strangely menacing-looking. Within this cloud is the silhouette of a black creature travelling at what looks like great speed towards the forest. Underneath the image is a word scratched so deeply it has almost created a hole in the page. The word is Sturmfalken. Does that mean "storm hawk"?

"Have you heard of the Sturmfalken?" I whisper, looking up at Raphael.

His head is hanging low, making it difficult to see his eyes. His hands are gripping the side of the desk.

"I think you have," I say quietly. "What do you know about this?"

"I don't know, Cassie, but there is something familiar about them." He examines the page. "But I can't think where I've seen them before. I've heard old folk tell tales of giant birdlike creatures swooping over the forest, but I'm sure it's just superstition."

The cherub starts to stir in my arms.

She lets out a piercing shriek and instinctively I put my hand over her mouth to hush her.

"Shush!" I whisper, my heart suddenly pounding. "We're trying to protect you."

She looks at me through eyes that are not human – a colour I have never seen before. In her eyes are all the jewels of the world: aquamarine and sapphire and emerald, somehow combined to create one unearthly hue. They are strangely beautiful, and round, like an owl's, and framed as if with kohl. There's something about them that both unsettles and reassures me at the same time. In her eyes I see great strength, wisdom, and

27

perhaps a little fear too.

She begins to tremble in my arms and *my* fear disappears. I touch her head to reassure her. "Can you speak?" I ask, even though I know the answer. She doesn't say anything, but instead makes a soft cawing sound. "Please don't worry," I say. "I won't hurt you." She crawls closer to me, as if to become a part of me. She looks around the room, taking everything in. When her eyes fall back on me I smile at her, trying not to look worried. "I'll look after you," I say.

I want to learn more about the Sturmfalken and question Raphael further, but now with the cherub awake it doesn't feel right somehow. I shift her position on my knee. "I think we should put the book away for now," I say. "We don't want anyone else finding this, least of all Papa. He'd only worry."

Raphael slides the book back into its place on the shelf before returning to his chair.

We sit for some time, transfixed with the cherub, but like frightened new parents, not knowing quite what to do next.

Raphael cranes his neck to see what the storm is doing. "I'm going to have to go," he says. "I promised Father I wouldn't be long. Will you be all right until tomorrow?"

"Please don't go," I say, feeling a rising panic at the

thought of being left alone with the cherub.

"I have to. I'm sorry. If I don't, he'll come looking for me, and you know what happened last time."

How could I forget? Of course Raphael needs to go. I cringe as I remember how Mother treated his father the last time he came to the house.

"But please be careful if you have to go out," he says. "And keep her close by." He puts a hand on the cherub's head, and she makes a gentle mewing sound. "And don't leave her where Bram can get at her," he adds, smiling.

He gets up and rolls his shoulders as if they are troubling him. As he reaches the door, he stops and turns to me. I'm certain he wants to say something else, but he leaves without another word.

I tiptoe to my room, the cherub still in my arms, and look out of the window. As Raphael walks back to his cottage a shaft of winter sunlight settles on his retreating back, illuminating him slightly. He turns to wave before disappearing through his front door. The clouds, still swirling about our rock, are heavy and dark, but the storm has passed.

The cherub stirs. I sit on my rocking chair and settle her on my knee to take a better look at her. The feathers that cover her round baby-like body are beginning to fluff up as they dry, making her look larger than earlier.

Her feet and hands are bare, like those of a baby. The soft hair on her head, like her skin, feels as ancient and fragile as the Earth.

She turns her inquisitive face to me, and for a while we sit and study each other. She seems as interested in me as I am in her.

She stretches her wings out and I run my fingers along them, carefully untangling any storm-damaged tips. They are as soft as velvet, and are gleaming now, like the inside of a shell. They look too small for her to fly. But then how did she reach my room? I think of the eagle owl in the owlery and his vast wingspan, and the owls that circle our rock at night. Her wings are different to theirs, but she is so light, perhaps she is simply lifted by the wind. I softly blow on her to dry her feathers. She flutters her wings, as if testing them. She does not try to fly, but I wonder if and when she will.

Chapter Five

The doorbell rings, making me jump. We have bells all over the place – appropriated over the years from shipwrecks, abandoned farmhouses, and long-dead alpine cows – and their combined peal is deafening. Whenever a visitor pulls on the front door bell, all the bells in the house jump to attention, and the subsequent cacophony makes the house quake from the engine room in the basement all the way up to

Mother's music room.

"Answer that, Cassie!" Mother shouts from two floors above.

It will be the nurses. They're here, no doubt, to poke and prod poor Grandma.

The cherub is still preening herself on my knee. I know I can't leave her on her own with Bram prowling around, so I scoop her up, smooth down her wings, and wrap her close to my chest in an old shawl. Glancing sideways at myself in my wardrobe mirror I notice she is still clearly visible. I reach for another scarf and drape it round my neck, allowing it to fall over my front, hoping the loose fabric will help to conceal her.

I can't imagine she likes being trussed up this way, but she doesn't try to wriggle free. That strange feeling floods my body once more. Again it seems as if our two hearts are beating as one. It's disconcerting, as I can almost *hear* my heart pounding in my chest. I feel stronger too. Less fearful almost. I shake the feeling off. I must be imagining it.

One of the cherub's wingtips flicks up and protrudes above my scarf, tickling my chin, so I ease her further down until I'm certain she's completely hidden. She utters an odd little caw, and I peek under my scarf to check she is well. Her eyes are heavy, and it looks as if she's falling asleep, like a baby in her mother's arms. Of course I know she's not a baby, and I should probably be terrified holding something so peculiar so close – but I don't feel frightened. It almost feels like we belong together. Like two halves making more than one.

I decide to take the zip, to avoid running all the way down to the ground floor. Grandpa didn't have the patience to run up and down several storeys every day and designed our unusual lift "after too many glasses of schnapps", according to Mother. It isn't too dangerous if you're careful.

I step on to the round wooden platform, wrap one arm round the vertical pole that runs through the middle of it, and slide the other under the cherub. I release the lever with my chin and we plummet through the house, me pumping on the small foot brake to control the speed of our descent. The cherub makes a fearful shriek, and I pull her closer to reassure her. Despite our speed, I catch glimpses of life on each floor of the house – brief moments in time I might otherwise have missed: Emaline leaving the owlery with a small package under an arm and Bram at the dining-room table gnawing on something he probably shouldn't. I'm relieved to reach the ground floor without injuring myself and with the cherub still attached.

I wonder if I might be able to persuade the nurses to travel up to Grandma's room on the zip for speed. The steam cannon Grandpa designed for firing the platform back up through the house creates an even more terrifying experience than the freefall descent, so I'd be surprised if they agreed. Papa and I often travel up together, so I know it will take the weight of two people.

The doorbell rings again, and I am briefly deafened.

"Will someone answer the blasted door?" Mother bellows again from her music room.

I'm always amazed how sound travels up and down through our house. It must be something to do with the holes that Grandpa cut in every floor when the zip was built.

I heave open the heavy front door. Does Mother ever answer the door? I'm sure I'm the only one who does. It creaks horribly, and I make a mental note to oil its hinges.

The nurses, Frau Crunch and Frau Grind, are standing side by side on the doorstep. Their trap is parked behind them and their sturdy pony snorts in the cold morning air. Everyone calls them Crunch and Grind, but I'm sure these cannot be their real names.

"We are here to see Frau Engel," they say as one in deep voices, as they do every time they visit, like they've

Fledgling

never been here or met me before.

"Ah yes, hello," I say, trying to look bright. I'm sure they'll notice the strange bulge in front of me. I wrap my arms round me as if trying to protect myself from the icy air blowing in through the front door. But they barely look at me, clearly impatient to get in and out as quickly as possible. Everyone who visits always seems to be in a terrible rush to leave. "Come in," I say, stepping aside.

"Is she in her room?" they say once they are in and I have pushed the door closed behind them.

"Of course," I reply. "Would you like to take the zip? It'll be much quicker than the stairs."

They look at me as if I'm mad, and then at the little lift platform, waiting just a couple of feet away. And then back up at the long staircase looming in front of us. They know Grandma is three floors up. I can see they are tempted.

"Very well," one of them says. "It will save us the effort of carrying our bags all that way." She doesn't wait for agreement from the other one, who shrugs and pulls a face.

"If you say so," she says.

I know they're sisters, but I wonder now, looking at them, if they might be twins. They both have the same wavy brown hair, which today is tied up in matching tight buns, and deep-set eyes shaded by eyebrows that almost meet in the middle.

They shuffle towards the zip, flicking suspicious eyes in my direction, and step on cautiously. I notice them glancing up at the hole in the ceiling above before squeezing closer together, almost nose to nose, their large leather bags wedged between their heavy brogues.

"I just have to generate some steam," I say casually, trying not to frighten them, but beginning to worry this is not a good idea. I grab the large metal handle on the wall next to the platform and start pumping it up and down vigorously. I hear the hiss of steam as it's drawn from the boiler in the engine room below to the cylinder just beneath Crunch and Grind's feet. The needle on the small brass pressure gauge flickers to green, indicating it's ready to go. I let go of the handle, release the brake on the platform and jump back. When it's just me on there, I usually shoot up three floors in only a few seconds, but now the platform moves upwards slowly, in an almost stately fashion. The nurses rise through the hallway towards the narrow cut-out above.

I trot up the stairs, noticing how the cherub feels almost weightless, and stop at each floor to wait for Crunch and Grind. Each time, as they rise up past me, they ignore me, their faces set in unreadable frowns, their knuckles white from clinging to the handle that wraps round the pole.

It's strange to see them like this, knowing how feared they are around Edenburg. I hear they are good at what they do and relied upon for the conditions that don't need to be dealt with in the sanatorium. The relocation of joints is a particular speciality of theirs, with dislocations common among the forestry workers and huntsmen. I've heard stories of woodcutters weeping for their mothers as they're pinned down by Crunch or Grind while the other pops a shoulder or ankle joint back into place, apparently unmoved by their victims' pleas for mercy. They also deliver babies, stitch up wounds, and pay weekly visits to people like Grandma who are too old, ill or stubborn to be treated elsewhere.

When I reach Grandma's floor, I stand and wait at the open lift shaft, ready to help them off. They rise up through the hole in the floor, heads held high, faces still set in fixed frowns. As soon as the platform is level with the floor, I lean in and slam the lever shut, allowing the platform to come to a gentle stop. I notice how their hands are shaking as I help them off, one at a time.

As we enter Grandma's room they tut at the sight of the pump.

"Still got that antique attached?" one of them says.

"Yes," I reply. "If it takes her pain away, I'm not going to disconnect it."

"Humph," says Crunch or Grind. "It should be in a museum, not wired into a person." They complain about it every time they come, and every time I ignore them. They look around the room disapprovingly. "She," Crunch or Grind says, nodding in the direction of Grandma, "should be in the sanatorium. This is no place for someone as sick as her." I know that being in the hospital is the last thing Grandma wants, but I say nothing. I bustle around her bed instead, trying to feel useful. I want her to know I'm here.

Grandma's chest is rising and falling gently, almost in time with the pump's bellows. I lean towards her and whisper into her ear. "Grandma, are you awake? The nurses are here."

"Oh God," she groans, peeling her eyes open to look at me. Every time she opens her eyes now, a little more of the bright blue I remember so well as a child seems to have been washed away, leaving lifeless opal pools behind. Her voice is barely audible, but I spot a small movement in her hand, as if she's trying to wave the nurses away. I slip my hand into hers. As I do so she whimpers. "Sorry, darling," she whispers through cracked lips, "it's just that everywhere hurts so much now."

I step back, fighting away tears, as the nurses prepare to move her into a new position. Every time they visit, I plead with them to leave her as she is, but they say it has to be done. "The last thing she needs on top of everything else is a bedsore," they say each time. "And she needs a wash," one says now, curling her nose.

I surreptitiously tweak the pump up another notch, leave Grandma's room and go out to the staircase, hearing the door slam behind me. I sink down on to the top step and run my fingers along the weave of the old threadbare carpet. It was probably a vibrant red once, possibly with a bold pattern, but now it has faded to a dull brown, with parts so worn you can see through it to the floorboards below. A smell of stale tobacco is released as my fingers scratch at the ancient wool. I wrap my arms round the cherub. She's watching me from under the shawl through wide concerned eyes, and I lean down and kiss the top of her head.

I wish I could do more for Grandma. We all know she's dying, and that there's nothing we can do for her, apart from inflicting Crunch and Grind on her every week, and keeping the morphine pump topped up. It looks so barbaric, with its noisy bellows and clunky dials;

I'm surprised the nurses don't like it more.

Eventually I hear Grandma's door opening and I turn round to see Crunch or Grind sticking her head out. "She's all done," she shouts, assuming, perhaps, that I'm a little deaf.

I jump up and head back to Grandma's room. She looks more comfortable in recently puffed pillows and smells of carbolic soap.

"Thank you," I say, and they both nod.

"Just doing what she pays us to do," one of them says. "We'll be back in a week."

The other one plonks a large mixing bowl on Grandma's dressing table. "If she gets a bedsore, use this," she says.

I lean over the bowl and examine its contents. It appears to be full to the brim with a gloopy substance in a peculiar shade of green. How many bedsores do they expect Grandma to get?

"Useful for other wounds too," she says, her eyes slipping to her sister in a conspiratorial way.

I kiss Grandma goodbye after the nurses have left the room. "I'll come and see you later," I say, returning briefly to the giant bowl of gloop. "Let's hope you don't need all this. There's enough to treat a small army in here!"

"Indeed," Grandma says. "Let's hope so."

I don't offer Crunch and Grind another ride on the zip. Instead I accompany them down the staircase, trying to make conversation as we plod down together.

"That was some storm," I say.

"Ja," Crunch or Grind says.

"Did you get caught out in it?"

"Ja," replies the other.

"Do you have more visits to make today?"

"Ja," they reply together.

When we reach their trap, they clamber in at the same time, one on each side, a well-rehearsed routine, no doubt, to stop it from tipping over. Then, cracking their little whip, they head off down our helter-skelter road and back to the outside world.

Chapter Six

It is almost dark when Emaline rings the bell for dinner. I tuck the cherub into my old boot box and place a scarf over her. Having checked Bram isn't hiding in my room, I creep out.

Emaline has laid two places halfway down the long dining-room table facing each other – one close to the fire for Mother, and the other, opposite, for me. Papa must be delayed in München. The table seats twenty-four, but it's years since we've had more than three of us for dinner. Not since Grandpa died and Grandma became so ill. Bram is asleep on his back further down the table, his white-tipped paws thrown over his head, his soft belly rising and falling as he dreams. I take my seat and wait, wondering if the cherub will still be in my room when I return.

Mother floats into the room in a cloud of perfume and silk, her sequinned gown shimmering in the firelight, a hooded cloak billowing behind her. She continues past me and heads to the far end of the table, away from the fire, the light of the candles – and me. Her face is inscrutable.

"Pass me the bell, Cassie," she says, once she has arranged herself in a chair.

I pick up the little bell Emaline has left in Mother's usual place, slide my chair back, walk along the table and plonk it down in front of her. I return to my seat.

Mother inclines her head, as if to say thank you. Then she rings the bell and sits with a rod-straight back and expectant eyebrows as she waits for Emaline to appear.

Emaline eventually shuffles in, dressed as usual in her off-white apron. Her hair is tied roughly on top of her head with what looks like an old stocking. She has a basket of bread tucked under her arm.

"Ja?"

"Emaline, would you be a dear and make up my place here?"

A tight knot forms in my stomach and I feel my face redden. Is she trying to avoid me? I should be the one who is furious. Not her.

Emaline looks at me, and then at Mother. Sighing, she picks up Mother's wine glass and cutlery, limps the length of the table, and re-lays Mother's place. She reaches into her deep apron pocket and pulls out a dusty bottle of wine. With strong hands she twists the cork out and pours a glassful for Mother before heading back to the kitchen. She hasn't gone far when Mother rings her bell again. Emaline stops and stands for just a few seconds, clenching and unclenching her fists. She turns and walks back to Mother.

"Ja?"

"Thank you, Emaline, that will be all," Mother says. "I don't think I had dismissed you, but now I have. You may return to the kitchen."

Emaline looks for a second as if she might throw something at Mother – possibly a punch – but then she turns away and leaves. I know how little work there is in this area these days, now that so many of the grander houses have been sold. Does Emaline have a family to feed? A mother to take care of? It occurs to me how little I know about her.

Mother and I sit in silence for a while. She sips her wine as I watch the rise and fall of Bram's belly. He's soaking up the warmth from one of the giant silver candelabras. I worry that hot wax might fall on to him at any minute, but he seems unperturbed.

I glance at Mother. She's staring at one of the small leaded windows with wide eyes and blinks heavily. If I didn't know her better, I'd think she was trying not to cry.

Eventually Emaline returns with a soup tureen. She sets it down next to Mother, and with a large pewter ladle slops a mound of grey mixture into her bowl.

Mother scrutinises it carefully. As Emaline approaches me, she calls after her.

"Emaline, dear, would you mind telling me what this is?" She slides the mixture around her bowl with her spoon.

"Leberknödel," Emaline replies. Liver dumpling soup.

It's not my favourite dish, and certainly not Mother's, but I believe it's popular among the locals when cooked well. Does Emaline deliberately try to annoy Mother? I'm certain I'd asked her to prepare a Leberkässemmel, but maybe she'd forgotten or misheard me.

"Ah, good, my favourite," Mother says brightly, perhaps noticing the narrowing of Emaline's eyes. She takes a sip of wine and puts her spoon down on the table.

Emaline slops a ladleful of Leberknödel into my bowl and leaves the room.

"Oh God," Mother says when she's gone, examining the contents of her bowl, "why is it so grey, Cassie?"

I shrug and taste a small spoonful. The liver is rubbery and a little difficult to swallow, but it isn't terrible. The greyness is probably just caused by the mushrooms.

"It tastes better than it looks," I say.

Mother lights a cigarette and inhales deeply.

I hear the clatter of horses' hooves and my heart leaps. Papa must be home from München! Minutes later the front door creaks open noisily, and Papa and Brutus clomp up the stairs towards us. They burst in in a flurry of boots, fur coats and an armful of parcels. With his wet hair and giant beard Papa looks wild. Brutus's eyebrows are heavy with rain, and his shaggy coat is sodden. He shakes, his ears slapping against his head, spraying muddy water over the table.

Mother glares at Papa and I wonder if they have had another argument.

"Hello, Cassie darling," Papa says, planting a cold bristly kiss on my forehead. "And hello, Gabriele," he adds, almost as an afterthought, bowing in Mother's direction. He does not try to kiss her.

Bram wakes and stretches and stares with unblinking eyes at Brutus.

Brutus whimpers and hides behind Papa's legs.

Papa throws his coat on to the back of one of the battered leather chairs at the fireside and lifts the bellows from the hook on the wall.

"Emaline," he calls, vigorously pumping air on to the dying embers. "Pour me some of that delicious soup, will you?"

I'm relieved he's back – but of course having Papa home brings its own problems.

Chapter Seven

I return to my room shortly after nine o'clock and find the cherub sitting up in the boot box, waiting for me. I rush to her and scoop her up. She sinks into my arms and I gasp as light-headedness briefly overwhelms me. She seems to be drawing the breath from my body, but I have no wish to stop her. I know I should put her down but I can't. She seems to be drinking me in. Taking something from me that she needs. My legs feel weak and I stagger to my bed and sit down until the feeling has passed.

She seems brighter than earlier, and more alert.

"What did you do just then?" I say, smoothing her feathers.

She whirrs her wings so they stick up again at all angles.

"Can you speak?" I say, wondering if there might be a way for us to communicate.

She raises her eyebrows just slightly and looks away before beginning to groom herself with her hands, pulling at her feathers, arranging them neatly again.

I hear Papa calling my name. He sounds excited about something. I put the cherub back in the boot box, close my door carefully and head towards his room.

As I reach his door, he leaps out at me, grinning. Brutus follows him out, his tail thudding loudly against the dark wood panelling.

"Cassie!" Papa says. "I have something to show you!" He looks older than ever, his wild hair more grey than brown, his smiling eyes framed by deep worry lines.

"I'm a bit busy, Papa. Can I look later?"

"It won't take a minute," he says, and with a flourish plucks something from behind my ear. It was my favourite trick when I was younger, and he amazed me every time with his sleight of hand. But today his hands are shaking and whatever he was clutching falls to the floor and rolls down the corridor towards the gloom at the far end. The animal heads that line both walls watch with indifference as it passes. Brutus bounds down the corridor after it, snatches it up and lopes back towards us with it in his mouth.

"Drop, Brutus!" Papa says, holding out his hand, and Brutus spits the slimy object into his palm. Papa wipes it on his stained, saggy trousers, and I wonder how often he changes them. His bare feet, protruding from the falling hems, are grey and bony, and cold-looking.

"Ta-da!" he says, revealing something shiny between his thumb and forefinger. It's a glass eyeball.

"It's lovely, Papa," I say, glancing back towards my room. Did I imagine that shriek? It's probably just Bram, having fun with a bird. "Is it for an owl?" I say. I know he's planning his next taxidermy project, a barn owl he found dead in the forest last week.

"No, Cassie!" He rolls his eyes. "This is a cat's eye. You of all people should know that."

"And do you have a cat in mind for it?"

"Of course I do, darling – it's for Ludwig. One of his eyes popped out last week. I think it must have rolled under the floorboards – or somewhere." He glances around the corridor as if the missing eye might suddenly reappear. "Anyway, come and see what I bought in München." He heads back into his bedroom and I follow him in reluctantly.

His small bed is unmade. It's been years since Mother banished him from their bedroom. She said she couldn't stand the smell of the preserving chemicals he used on the animal skins. She said he reeked of the stuff.

Ludwig, his first ever taxidermy project, is curled up at the end of the bed, ears pricked, one eye staring up at us, the other an empty cavity. His fur is threadbare, but apart from that and the missing eye he is recognisable as a cat.

Emaline tried to explain Papa's love of taxidermy once. We were in the kitchen and she was making bread. I was sitting at the end of the table watching her pummel a lump of dough. "It's because he can't bury them," she'd said. "Saw his friends churned into the earth in the war. Can't bear to see anything buried again." I wondered how she knew this. He never talked to me about the war. Did he really see his friends "churned into the earth"? And why had he told Emaline about it? But I know she often hauls him up from his armchair in the early hours after he's fallen asleep in front of the fire, an empty bottle of schnapps rolling at his feet. I've seen her help

51

him along the corridor past my room late at night, when I should be asleep, seeing him safely to bed. Maybe he said something then.

"Look at these, Cassie," Papa says, clearing a space on the bed for me. I perch next to him and he passes me a small wooden tray. It's divided into sections containing pairs of wobbling eyes of varying sizes and colours. From a distance it might look like a box of chocolates.

"Made in Berlin by the most skilled craftsmen in Germany," he says, scooping an eye out and peering at it. "The detail is incredible – look." He holds it out to me and I'm briefly intrigued. The teardrop-shaped pupil is dark, almost black, and the amber iris with tiny lines of brown makes it look just like a real eye. "It's for a fox," Papa whispers.

"Do we have a fox that needs stuffing, Papa?"

"Of course not, but if we ever do, I have the eyes for it."

"They're terrific," I say, smiling as I get up. "I'd better go. I'm just running an errand for Grandma. She'll be waiting for me." It's a small lie, but I know with Papa I'm unlikely to be caught out.

"I'm sure she can wait, Cassie. I just need you to give me a hand with something." He drops to his knees and pulls a box out from under the bed.

"I've hidden this lot from *you-know-who*," he says with a conspiratorial wink as he plonks it on to the bed. He often refers to Mother this way. "I just need a hand getting it all into the workshop without her noticing." He reaches under the bed again. "There's a couple more under here."

We pile boxes up on the bed. He rips one of them open, like a child unwrapping a gift on Christmas Day, and pulls out a large jar. "*This* is formaldehyde," he says, twisting open the lid and inhaling deeply. The pungent smell fills the room, and I bury my nose in my sleeve.

"You need to grow a stronger stomach, Cassie, if you want to master the art of taxidermy," he says, pulling a face at me. I bite my lip and say nothing. He pulls out another smaller jar containing a powder, opens the lid, and shakes the contents. "And this is borax," he announces, "for preserving an animal's skin. Marvellous stuff." He replaces the lid and puts it back in the box.

I hate his hobby, and I hate how he displays some of his projects – lumpy beavers and grotesquely deformed rabbits – around the house. He took me to an exhibition of taxidermy at the Glaspalast in München once. The creations on display there were magnificent: tiny mice dressed as ballerinas, a rabbit taking a bath, and even a grand-looking owl dressed as a military general.

They were quite different to Papa's creations. But he is improving. Perhaps one day he will make some money from it.

He picks up a small red glass bottle with a cork stopper. "And this, Cassie," he whispers, looking up at me from under his brows, "is white arsenic. To keep creepy-crawlies out of the skin." The label features a prominent skull and crossbones, and the word *Poison* is emblazoned in bold print underneath. I'm relieved he doesn't pull the stopper out.

"Should we keep that somewhere safe? Locked away?" I say, worrying whether Papa should be in possession of a lethal poison such as this.

"Good point, Cassie," he says. "Wouldn't want your mother getting hold of it. Heaven knows what she'd do with it." He returns it carefully to the box.

He piles me high with boxes and we tiptoe together along the corridor, past the watching heads and my bedroom. The door is closed and it seems quiet in there. Brutus whimpers outside it for a second, but when I whistle he trots after us, glancing briefly backwards.

Once inside the owlery I kick the door closed and we stack the boxes up outside Papa's small workshop. He unlocks the door with a noisy clunk and stoops as he leads us in through the low doorway. The smell of chemicals overwhelms me, as it always does. We haul the boxes in and stack them on the *billot de boucher*, the old butcher's table Grandpa salvaged from a flea market in Rothenburg. An amber-coloured liquid has dribbled down the Paris butcher's insignia at the front of the block, highlighting the smart-looking lettering. Papa reaches across the bench and pulls open a tiny drawer in the apothecary cabinet at the back of the block, and places a pair of brown eyes inside. He slides out the blank yellowing label from the little brass frame at the front of the drawer and, picking up a pen, carefully writes *Fox eyes* in miniscule script on it, before slipping it back into place. He opens the next empty drawer and repeats the process for the cats' eyes.

"Do you need me for anything else, Papa?" But he's deep in concentration and appears not to hear me.

My attention is drawn to a stuffed macaque monkey propped up against a pamphlet on the shelf high above the butcher's block. The creature is staring at the opposite wall through whiskered grey eyes framed with black. With its downturned mouth, threadbare fur and wide scar running the length of its abdomen, it looks a picture of eternal misery. I wonder where Papa got it from; I haven't seen it before. I peer at the pamphlet, thinking it should probably be in the library. It's old and yellowing, with curling edges and handwritten lettering scrawled across the front. I can just make out the word *unfurling* in the dim light. It must be something to do with Papa's taxidermy. He notices me looking at it, but assumes it's the monkey that has intrigued me.

"Isn't it a beauty!" he exclaims, clapping his hands together. "This monkey is the perfect example of the art of taxidermy, Cassie. Without people like me this creature would be lost to the world forever."

I back towards the door, desperate for fresh air. "Papa, I think I need to lie down," I say.

I race upstairs to my bedroom and find the cherub where I left her. A horrible thought occurs to me. Would Papa be tempted to preserve the essence of *her* species if he knew about her? Would he hook out her intestines and steep her in formaldehyde?

She's transfixed by the stuffed owl I keep on the shelf above my bed. It's bizarrely dressed in a velvet smoking jacket – a present from Papa for my twelfth birthday. According to Mother, he spent weeks in his workshop sprucing it up for me. She says he bought the velvet for the jacket from a shop in München and spent hours choosing the brass buttons from the expensive haberdasher on Maximilianstraße. He made the tiny leather boots himself and polished them until they gleamed. It's probably the best thing he's ever created, and he gave it to me.

"It's dead, don't worry," I say to the cherub. I reach up and take it down and lie it on the bed next to her so she can see how lifeless it is.

Chapter Eight

The next day the sky has cleared, and the air feels almost warm. Grandma has asked for mushroom soup for lunch, so I promised to forage for some from the forest. If a bowl of creamy Pouzar mushroom soup won't entice her to eat, then nothing will. I should be there and back in time for lunch.

I fling my bedroom window open and look out to see what the day is doing, and spot Emaline heading into town with a basket slung over her arm. I run down to the kitchen with the cherub, hoping to find something she might eat; she must be hungry after everything that's happened. I tempt her with breadcrumbs soaked in water, a glass of warmed milk, and even a little sauerkraut. But she looks at me as if she hasn't a clue what I'm trying to do. Perhaps Raphael was right about her not needing food. She doesn't appear to be withering. In fact, she seems to be getting stronger and heavier with every hour that passes. She definitely looks a little plumper and her eyes are even brighter than yesterday. I remember what I read in the illuminated manuscript. *A cherub on Earth draws sustenance from the chosen host, for love is the food that nurtures them.* I wish I knew what it meant.

Mother mentioned at breakfast that she would like her roof opened today. When she built her music room, she designed a domed copper roof that opens up when required, like a tulip unfurling in spring. She often asks me to open it when she wishes to sing to the sky. The open roof is quite a sight, and often causes the townsfolk to stop and stare even more at our unusual house.

I strap the cherub to my chest and fly down the zip to the engine room to open the roof and do my usual jobs before I go out.

I go to the boiler first – a vast cylindrical iron furnace I feed with wood every morning. I never let it go out, even in the height of summer when the house is less chilly, as it supplies us with hot water and creates the steam for the zip. I choose the largest log I can manage, crank open the iron door and throw it in.

I decide to quickly oil the cogs before I start the process of opening the roof. I pick up the oil tin, climb on to the workbench and stretch up to reach the network of pulleys, cogs and wires that are spread over the wall, wishing as always that I was taller. This is one of my many jobs in here: oiling cogs, untangling wires, replacing worn parts and tightening bolts to keep the mechanics of the house running smoothly. Grandpa said the house would seize up in days if I let this daily maintenance slip. Using a pipette, and being careful not to spill anything on to the cherub's head, I squeeze glistening drops of oil into all the moving parts I can reach. I wish Mother or Papa showed more interest in the workings of the house, but I've learned it's just easier to do these things myself. I tap one of the glass-fronted dials and watch with satisfaction as the needle flickers into life.

Everything seems to be running as it should, so I climb down from the bench and head to an iron box containing a giant reel of thick steel cable tucked away in the corner of the room. Grandpa told me once it's the type you'd see in a shipyard to secure a ship to the quay. Beside the reel is a tall timber strut flanked by two upright mahogany and brass ship's wheels – the mechanism that operates Mother's roof. I heave on one of the wheels, using all my strength to turn it 180 degrees. Once it has clunked into place, I take hold of the second wheel. This one is always the stiffer of the two, and I brace myself for the effort. I tie a knot in my dress to avoid catching it in the machinery and use my whole body weight to turn it. It's even trickier today with the cherub strapped to my front, watching what I'm doing with interest. The wheel finally clicks into position and the process of opening the roof begins. It will take some time for all the sections to fully retract.

I suddenly remember Raphael's concern about me leaving the house, but I can't stay cooped up here until I've worked out what to do with the cherub. And I promised Grandma I'd find some mushrooms for her soup – it's the only thing I can think of to make her feel better. Could there really be anything out there looking for the cherub? Raphael's probably being overly cautious, but still I hunt about for a suitable weapon to take with me, just in case. I rummage in Grandpa's old toolbox, and spot his crowbar. I turn it over in my hand.

It's solid and heavy, but not too unwieldy. I decide it will do, tuck it into my belt and head down the rock and towards the forest, feeling just a little apprehensive.

Chapter Nine

I reach my favourite clearing in the forest, place my basket on an old tree stump and scan the snow-capped treetops. I wrap my arms more tightly round the cherub, already wishing I had listened to Raphael's warning. I don't know what it is, but something feels different out here today. It's almost as if I'm being watched; the forest is too quiet. The cherub growls. The hairs on the back of my neck prick. I glance around – one hand on her and the other clutching the crowbar in my belt.

Eventually, deciding my imagination is getting the better of me, I tuck the crowbar away and crouch down to cut some tender-looking mushrooms with my paring knife. A chill passes through my body. I look up but see nothing strange. The cherub growls again.

I quickly stuff what I can into my basket. I need to get the cherub home. I shouldn't have brought her with me.

Her growling becomes more urgent.

My heart pounds, and I reach for the crowbar again.

The temperature plummets.

A violent shriek shatters the air just behind me.

I run.

Something jabs at the back of my neck.

I scream.

Out of the corner of my eye I see the wing of a large birdlike creature. Something tugs at my hair and I scream again, trying to hit it with my crowbar. A long curved beak pecks at my face.

It sniffs loudly, almost as if it's trying to smell me. I wrap my arms protectively round the cherub, overwhelmed by the bird's stench. It smells as if it's been dead for months, but it is clearly very much alive. The cherub shrieks and I feel the creature's hot stinking breath on my cheeks. It pulls at my dress, pulling me upwards. My feet leave the ground and I kick out violently, screaming and squirming and thrashing so much that it drops me.

As I land heavily on the forest floor, I feel the creature's weight on my back and its sharp beak tears at my hair again. Warm liquid seeps down my neck. I must be bleeding.

The cherub is still.

"Are you hurt?" I cry as I thrash and swipe above my head.

She screams.

A feeling of immense strength surges through me and spreads down my arms and legs.

The cherub roars.

I roar.

I spin round, somehow grabbing hold of one of the creature's talons and slam it into the ground.

I scream.

I scream in a rage I cannot control.

I scream.

I scream again.

My throat is on fire.

And then the world becomes dark.

★

Some time later I find myself on my knees, the cherub still tied tightly to my chest. I have no idea how long I have been like this, but my legs are stiff with cold. I look in horror at the bloodied mess before me and put my hands over my face.

Did I do this?

What have I done?

I hear shouting from somewhere nearby. It is Raphael. My heart sinks; he cannot see me like this.

"Cassie!" he cries, stumbling on fallen branches as he rushes towards me. "Cassie, are you all right? I heard you from my house!"

He stops dead as he sees me and what remains of the creature lying in smithereens beside me.

"Did *you* do this?" he says.

I nod, sobbing. "But I don't know what happened. Something came over me. Something I've never felt before." I hang my head.

I watch as blood from the creature sinks into the damp forest floor. Feathers and bones still lie scattered among the detritus of twigs and rotting leaves. The sun emerges from behind a cloud and illuminates a shard of bone. I pick it up hesitantly and turn it over.

"Raphael, this looks like glass," I say, dropping it to the ground as if it's on fire.

He picks up another piece. "It does," he says. "But that's impossible." He holds it up in the sunlight and examines it. I have never seen him look so grim. "Is the cherub hurt?" he says. "Are you hurt?"

I examine her carefully. I can't see any sign of injury. "We're both fine," I say, shaking my cape out, showering hundreds of tiny splinters of glass to the forest floor.

"You'll have to burn that," Raphael says. "It's covered in blood. Your mother will think you've murdered someone."

I look at it. He's right. And it's not just my cape that's covered in the remains of the bird. I put my hands to my cheeks. They feel stiff and tight. "Do I have its blood on my face?" I ask in horror.

"You might need a wash," he says. "And I also think you should close your mother's roof."

"Might there be more of them?" I say, horrified. "Do you think they'd try to get into the house?"

"There could be," he says, squinting up at the sky. "This may have been a scout, sent ahead of the others—"

"A scout?" I cry. I'm more certain than ever he's hiding something from me. "How do you know this was a scout?"

"I can't explain, Cassie. I just think there might be more. You have to trust me." He turns away, picks up my crowbar and starts to hack at the ground. "I'll bury this one."

I move towards him to see his face, but he turns away from me again.

"Just go, Cassie!" he pleads. "You need to close the roof."

Chapter Ten

I stumble home, clinging to the cherub, tripping over exposed tree roots and slipping on frozen puddles. Mother's roof is wide open. Her voice rises through the giant panels and soars like a golden eagle towards the distant Alps. She's singing the "Queen of the Night" aria from *The Magic Flute*. I hate it. I know every bar, every note, every inflection in her voice too well, having heard it rehearsed over and over again for as long as

I can remember.

The cherub, bouncing about in my arms, suddenly starts to sing. It's so quiet to begin with I almost don't notice at first, but then I realise she's singing in time with Mother! Something about her peculiar timbre sends a shiver down my spine so I keep running towards the house, my head low, trying to block her out. Then Mother's singing stops and the cherub falls silent once more.

I haul myself up the side of our rock using the winch, rather than following the long and laborious helter-skelter road, feeling safer inside the cage's iron bars. Emaline should still be in Edenburg. I pray that Papa is asleep so I can slip into the house unnoticed.

I sneak in through the engine-room door and head towards the boiler. I can't believe I'll be able to clean all this blood from my clothes, but I cannot let Emaline see them like this. I pull my cape off and open the boiler door. Poised in front of the open furnace, my hand shielding the cherub from the heat, I pause. I look at my cape, feeling the velvet soft beneath my fingers. It was from one of Papa's shopping trips to München. Mother had been furious when he'd returned home with it. She'd thrown a bottle of perfume at him and, intoxicated, he'd failed to duck. A slim scar remains on his forehead to this day. The cape *is* a little showy, but I still love it. I let it fall to the floor and with shaking hands, lie the cherub on it while I undo the fiddly buttons on my stained dress, and throw that into the boiler instead. Mother will be pleased to see it gone.

I remember I'm supposed to be closing the roof. I should have done that first, as it takes so long for all the sections to close. I return the wheels to their original position and lock them into place. I cannot believe one of those creatures would dare to fly into Mother's music room. I almost pity any that try.

The putrid smell of the bird is on my skin and in my nostrils. I cautiously sniff my hands. They stink of rotting flesh. Desperate for fresh air, I run to the door, and as I pull it open a gust of wind almost throws me off my feet. I slam it shut again and scoop the cherub up and pick up my basket and cape.

In just my chemise and stockings, I quickly take the mushrooms to the pantry, praying Emaline won't return home unexpectedly, before running up the stairs two steps at a time to my room, one hand dragging the cape behind me and the other clinging to the cherub. Papa is snoring in his room, and I know that Brutus won't come to see me. He never leaves Papa's side.

I dart into my room and drop my cape on the floor

before tucking the now-sleeping cherub into the old boot box. I wish I'd tossed my cape into the boiler after all, but it's too late for that now. I'll just have to hide it somewhere no one will find it. I think of the large leather trunk next to the cabinet of curiosities down the corridor. My great-grandmother's old gowns are stored in there, alongside other assorted items. It was my dressing-up box when I was younger, and I'm sure no one looks in it any more.

I open my door, creep along the corridor, wincing as the floorboards creak noisily under my footsteps. I crouch next to the trunk, jiggle the brass latch and open the lid. The acrid smell of mothballs billows up from the chest and I choke as the harsh chemicals hit the back of my throat. Grandma must have put them here years ago to protect the fragile fabrics from hungry moths. I shove my cape in and bury it under a decaying roll of lace and an old parasol. I tiptoe back to my room and close the door firmly behind me.

I feel I should do something with the cherub, but I don't know what. She's still sleeping soundly, as if unaware of what just happened in the forest. I decide to head to the bathroom.

Running the bath is a slow and noisy process, and I pace around the room as it fills. Eventually I sink into the deep, hot water and rub myself all over with a bar of lavender soap and Papa's scrubbing brush, touching my neck carefully where the bird pecked me. When I am certain I have removed all traces of the bird, I jump out, grab a stiff towel from the hot pipe, wrap it round myself and run down the corridor back to my room. I stand in front of my wardrobe mirror and crane my neck to examine my wounds. They really don't look too bad.

Papa is still snoring. I wonder if the screaming will start soon – that terrible thing we call his sleep terrors. I quickly pull on a clean dress, my nimble fingers swiftly doing up the tiny ivory buttons, so I can run to him if he needs me.

I look down at the cherub and my heart swells. Is this how a mother feels about her child? I lift her up and hold her close. As I do so that strange feeling floods my body again. The cherub curls up in my arms and we sit together for some time. I breathe her in. She smells of nuts and cloves and sweet almonds. I lean down and kiss her soft head. My kiss wakes her, and she looks up at me. She's vibrating gently, as if purring.

Feeling a little light-headed, I find a clean shawl, carefully strap her back on to my chest, and head for the library. I need to look at that book again.

Chapter Eleven

I open the door to the owlery and step inside. Something has changed in here. It takes me a moment to realise what it is.

The owls have all rotated by 180 degrees, and are now facing the forest. It's perfectly possible for anyone with the keys to the cases to spin their plinths round, but the only other person who knows where they are kept is Emaline, and this doesn't seem like the sort of thing she'd do.

The cherub wakes. She makes the strangest sound – part vibration, part cry – almost like the call of an animal in a trap. The volume rises. I put my hands over my ears, realising with horror that the shrieking is coming not just from the cherub, but from the owls too. I want to run away, but my feet feel glued to the floor. An overwhelming pressure wraps round my body. My head feels like it's in a vice. I struggle to draw breath.

And then, as quickly as it began, the noise stops. The pressure round my body is released and my feet are freed from their grip on the floorboards. I stagger backwards against the wall, breathing in and out deeply to calm myself. The cherub looks at me, as if to check I am well. I pull her close and feel our hearts beat faster and stronger than ever. The sensation takes my breath away and I sink to the floor.

Eventually I clamber back to my feet and stagger across the owlery, gripping the display cases for support as I go. As soon as I get into the library, I close the door behind me and sit for a while at the desk until my breathing has returned to normal, trying to make sense of what just happened.

I wonder if the feeling of being squeezed and unable to move was something to do with my fear. I've heard

75

how people can freeze when terrified. Was this what happened to Papa in the war? Was the fear he felt then so bad it made him like he is now?

I find the book I'm looking for easily as Raphael had left it slightly protruding from the others. I lie it carefully on the desk, worrying about its spine cracking or its pages falling out. I find the place we had been looking at yesterday. It feels like so long ago now. I flick the switch on the old desk lamp and a dim light settles on to the page.

I wish Raphael was here now. What must he think of me, having done such a terrible thing? But what could I do? Let it kill me?

I examine the sketch of the giant birdlike creature. The thing that attacked me looks quite like the one here. It's impossible to get an idea of its size from this sketch, but the bird's curved yellow beak and sharp talons are the same as those that clawed at my neck. I turn the page, desperate to find another explanation.

Two scribbled, encircled words I hadn't noticed yesterday grab my attention. *Fauliges Fleisch*. Putrid flesh. Is this referring to the creature's smell? I think of my efforts to scrub myself clean with Mother's expensive soap. I sniff my hands. The stink still lingers, despite me having washed so carefully.

I reread the phrase about love being the food that nurtures a cherub. Is it possible the term "host" doesn't refer to the angels, but to something quite different? I look down at her, at her round belly and glistening skin, and wonder.

I hear Mother call my name from above. Sighing, I tuck the cherub into the cavity under the desk and race through the owlery, keeping my eyes to the floor, not daring to look round. I run up the spiral staircase, throw the door open and burst into the music room.

Mother is standing, not quite red-faced, but more flushed than normal, in the centre of the room, staring up.

"Cassie," she says. "My roof has closed."

I look up and shrug. "I'll take a look in the engine room," I say. "There might be a problem with the mechanics." I back towards the door.

"If you would," she says, wafting me away with her hand. "It's such a wonderful day. It would be a shame to waste it."

I nod as I head out of the room.

"And have you got rid of the owls yet?"

My heart sinks. "No, not yet." I turn to face her. "I just have a feeling we should keep them. Why do you want to get rid of them?"

"I thought I'd made that perfectly clear," she says, waving a hand towards the small pile of Papa's boxes under a window. "And they give me the creeps."

"But you never go in the owlery," I say. I don't want to tell her they often give me the creeps too, but even after what just happened, I still couldn't live without them.

"That is not the point," she says. "Just knowing they're there is enough. It isn't normal, Cassie, to have a room full of dead owls in one's house. I simply wish them gone. Is that too much to ask?"

I don't think she's ever worried about how *normal* we are before. "I'll have a think about where to put them," I say, knowing I have no intention of doing any such thing.

I run back to the owlery. The owls have rotated again, back to their usual orientation. Worrying I'm losing my mind, I head into the library and slam the door behind me. I crawl under the desk, lift the cherub out and return to the book.

On the next page is a reference to another book: *Damman's Rules for Taxidermy: The Arte of Preserving the Owle for the Divination of Celestial Energie*. I decide to hunt for it in the section entitled ALL THINGS FEATHERED. I find it after a short hunt – a tiny volume nestled next to a brown leather-bound book on the owls of the Bratvian Forest. I pull it out and place it on top of the giant book still open on the desk.

I have just started reading it when Emaline rings the bell for lunch. I quickly close it and return it to the bookshelves, deciding to come back to it when I have done my jobs. I glance out of the window and down towards Raphael's cottage and wonder if he returned home safely from the forest.

Chapter Twelve

That night I wake to the distant sound of the grandfather clock preparing to announce the hour. After much groaning and grinding, it spits out two chimes before clunking into silence again. I swear under my breath. I've been struggling to sleep, worrying that Raphael didn't get home. I've already climbed out of bed twice to check he returned safely, hoping to see a light in his room. But each time I'd looked, his cottage was in darkness. I know he always sleeps with a lit candle by his side.

What if there were more of them out there?

I lie awake but unmoving, listening to the creaking of the house as it settles into the night.

I reach out for the cherub – I hadn't been able to resist taking her into bed with me – and realise she isn't there any more. My heart misses a beat.

The strangest sensation fills my room. It's a little like the vibration I felt in the owlery earlier – but this time my hair crackles as if I'm surrounded by static electricity.

I barely dare breathe, let alone go and investigate. I lie still for a while longer, my blankets over my nose, my eyes tightly closed.

The static electricity seems to ebb and flow, and as it briefly subsides I force my eyes open.

I see the cherub straight away, looking like a very different creature to the one I took to bed just a few hours ago. She is perched at the end of my bed, sitting upright, just like a baby – with the soles of her tiny feet pressed together, her hands resting on her knees. She is watching me, looking oddly grown-up, despite being so small. Her wide-set eyes are gleaming and her wings are outstretched. Her feathers are groomed and pristine.

"What are you doing?" I whisper, not wanting to frighten her. "You'll freeze if you don't come back to bed." But she doesn't look cold. In fact, she's actually glowing, as if lit up from the inside. "And how did you get there?" I look at her wings, alive and vibrant, and wonder. Did she fly?

I climb out of bed, flinching as my feet meet the icy floorboards. Moonlight filters into the room through my half-drawn curtains.

"Is a storm coming?" I say, wondering if she was woken by a crack of thunder. It must be an electric storm. Living high up means we are often exposed to bizarre weather, but I have never experienced anything like this. Perhaps we have been hit by lightning—

I creep towards the window, pull the curtains back, jiggle the little latch, and push the window open. Standing on tiptoe, I lean out to see if I can spot a thunder cloud. Far below, our rock is glowing like a beacon, illuminated by the bright moon. I feel the gentle sway of the house and wonder if this is what it's like in the crow's nest of a ship. The motion used to frighten house guests who weren't used to it, and they'd often complain of seasickness. I grip the window frame and lean out further. As I do so, a sharp gust of wind tugs at my hair and whips it about my head.

I am suddenly yanked back away from the window and flung roughly on to my bed. The window slams shut, and the curtains are pulled closed, as if by an invisible hand.

The room is thrown into darkness. I hear a flap of wings and a sharp screech and a scraping at the window.

I stare with wild eyes into the darkness.

There is something out there.

Something is hovering just outside my room.

The windowpanes creak, as if they are being sucked from their leaded frames.

"Go away!" I try to scream. But I make no sound.

I grip my blankets so hard my fingers hurt.

There is a crash as whatever is outside throws itself at my window.

I scream again silently.

And then I smell it.

Fauliges Fleisch.

Putrid flesh.

This is the stench of the creature that attacked me in the forest. Raphael was right. There must be more of them.

I glance at the cherub. She is standing now and staring at the window. Her eyes are ablaze.

The vibration in the room intensifies and I try to cry out, but now I cannot even open my mouth.

I feel as if I am being crushed – as if the air is being

83

drawn from my body.

The room seems to spin and a flash of light explodes around me, and I am briefly blinded.

And then, as quickly as it started, it stops.

I breathe in a lungful of air.

Moonlight floods the room once more, and the vibration is gone.

The only sound is the crashing of my heart.

The cherub and I sit unmoving for some time. I glance at her and she looks back at me.

"Did you do that?" I say eventually. I notice that the flames have left her eyes, and that they are now the colour of emeralds.

I climb down from my bed, creep back to the window and with shaking hands pull the curtains back again. In the distance a giant black bird swoops away from the house, down towards the forest.

Shivering, I climb back into bed.

I watch in amazement as the cherub spreads her wings, rises into the air and hovers for a second or so. Then she flies the short distance between us, her little wings flapping vigorously. I stretch my arms out towards her. She lands heavily on top of me, warm and baby-like – and, as I pull her to me, I begin to feel calm again.

"Was that a Sturmfalke?" I say, but of course she

doesn't reply. In fact, she looks exhausted and falls fast asleep in my arms. "How can you sleep now, after what just happened?" I say, breathing her in.

I arrange the covers around us, even though I suspect she doesn't need blankets to stay warm. But I lie awake, my heart still crashing, not daring to sleep. What invisible hand pulled me away from the window? Did the cherub somehow do *that*?

And who was she protecting? Me or herself?

Chapter Thirteen

As soon as it's light I send Raphael a message.

Where are you? I tap in a series of dits and dahs into my Morse code machine. I want to say more but I'm worried my shaking hands will make my message unintelligible.

Are you well? I add.

I climb back into the warmth of my bed, willing him to reply soon.

The cherub is sleeping so deeply I worry for a second she might be dead. But I see her chest suddenly rise and fall and breathe a sigh of relief. My heart swells as I remember how she lit up like a firecracker and flew to me, arms outstretched. I don't think I've seen anything more beautiful, or frightening, in my life.

I jump out of bed again and whip the curtains back, desperate to disperse all traces of the night from my room. The sun explodes in through the tiny glass panes, showering patterns of light over the walls. With a sinking heart I notice that the glass is smeared with what looks like saliva.

I stare back at the Morse code machine.

Please reply, Raphael!

I look out of the window again, down towards his cottage. Now that it's light, it's impossible to tell if his candle is still lit, but his window is shut.

I hear Emaline crashing about downstairs as she prepares breakfast. She's recently started serving kippers and eggs after Mother read in the *Münchener Ratsch-Kathl* that they were Queen Victoria's favourite breakfast. "If kippers are good enough for the Queen of England, then they will do for me," she had announced at the time, peering at me over the top of the paper. "They're good for your complexion too," she'd added pointedly. I can't stand the smell of them and usually feed mine to Brutus when no one's looking.

Something must be wrong with Raphael. It's just not like him not to reply. I pull a dress over my head and tug at my hair with my hairbrush, quickly rubbing in a handful of Macassar oil, and then unwind and rewind the roll of tape in the Morse code machine to check it isn't jammed. I'm just going to have to go and see him. I should be able to slip out before breakfast.

The smell of coffee wafts up through the floorboards, and I feel the gentle vibration of the heating system as it rattles into life for the day. I pull on my stockings and boots and feel the circulation return to my frozen feet.

The cherub is stirring, so I pick her up and tie her to me more tightly than yesterday, in case she tries to fly again. I rummage through my wardrobe and pull out the black velvet cape Mother bought me for wearing to the opera. It's too smart for daywear, but I can't think of anything else that will conceal her.

As I creep out of my room I hear the clackety sound of the armature on the Morse code machine readying itself to reveal a message. I rush back into my room and stand over it impatiently while it spits out a series of dits and dahs. Grabbing a pencil, I quickly decipher the message.

I'm well.

That's all he says but it's enough. He is alive!

Thanks, he adds.

I'm coming over, I reply, my heart racing.

I rush out of my room, my footsteps heavy with the extra weight of the cherub. She's wide awake and staring at me. She's smiling! I notice that her eyes are now as blue as sapphires. I smile back at her. "He's fine," I whisper, certain that she understands me.

"Cassie!!"

My heart sinks. It's Mother.

"Cassie!" Mother sings loud and high like the Queen of the Night. She rings her bell too – the little brass one she keeps on her bedside table. "Cassie!" she calls. "Ask Emaline to bring me breakfast in bed. I'm too fatigued to come down. I've had the most frightful night's sleep."

I hesitate briefly before deciding I didn't hear her. If Brutus can get away with selective hearing, then so can I. I jump on to the zip and shoot down through the house, pumping on the foot brake to slow it down, and leap off the platform a second before it comes to a grinding halt on the ground floor.

The cherub is looking about with interest as she bounces up and down in front of me. I leave the house through the engine room, to avoid having to grapple with the noisy front door. My jobs will have to wait until later.

I head out into the chilly morning air and climb into the rusting metal cage of the winch system. I pull down on the icy lever, and within seconds I'm crashing noisily and too slowly down the side of the rock.

I climb out at the bottom, step carefully down the rock's slippery lower levels, and follow the winding path towards the town and Raphael's cottage. Everywhere is covered in a light dusting of snow. As I reach the outskirts of town, the path changes to cobbles, and I kick the snow off my boots against a painted wooden signpost pointing back towards the forest. At the fork in the road by the Rathaus, I take Schulstraße past the Bäckerei, breathing in the smell of fresh bread. The clock on the Rathaus shows it is just past seven o'clock.

As I get closer to Raphael's, I begin to have second thoughts. I should have waited to hear back from him before racing out of the house. And what should I do if his father is home?

★

I find Raphael chopping logs in the little alley to the side of his cottage. He doesn't notice me at first, and I stand and watch him. I'm sure he has grown again since yesterday. He's only a year older than me but is already taller than Papa.

"Ah, hello!" he says when he finally notices me. He tosses a freshly split log on to the stack against the wall. "My friend, Cassie, slayer of all things feathered! Is everything all right?"

"I'm not a slayer," I say crossly. How can he joke like this when I've been awake all night worrying about him?

"I know you're not," he says, driving the axe into the chopping block. "It's just you did such a good job of obliterating that bird, you've made me a little nervous. I think perhaps you have hidden powers you haven't told me about."

"I don't know what happened," I say, wishing I didn't sound so grumpy. I stare at my feet. "You know that."

I sit down on the rough-hewn bench at the front of the cottage, and as Raphael joins me I worry it might give way under our combined weight. He stretches his legs and scuffs the ground with new leather boots. His lederhosen look new too. His father is always complaining about how quickly he's growing. He says it isn't normal for a boy to grow like that.

"I had to see you," I say. "I've been worrying about you, after what happened yesterday. About you having to clear it all up. Did you bury it?"

"You mustn't worry about me," he says. "I can look after myself. And, yes, I did. There wasn't much mess left after I'd finished with it. Just the odd feather." He seems transfixed with the cherub, but looks up at me briefly. "I've been worrying about *you* actually." He examines my neck. "It doesn't look too bad. Is it sore?"

"It's fine," I say. "It's nothing."

"And why were you so worried about me?" he says. "I wasn't the one attacked in the forest yesterday."

I bite my lip. "But you didn't come home last night. I thought something had happened to you."

"How do you know I didn't come home?" he says, grinning at me.

I take a deep breath. "Because I was awake half the night thinking about things. And I couldn't help checking to see if your candle was lit, to see if you were back – only once or twice, of course. I was worried you might have been attacked by another of those creatures."

"Oh no, it was nothing like that. I didn't come home because something happened in the forest after I buried the bird. I met someone who needed my help." He smiles at me. "But it's nice to know you're keeping an eye on me."

My cheeks burn as I grind a pine cone into the ground with one of my boots. "I was just worried after what happened. I'm not spying on you," I say. "And I think there *are* more of those creatures."

His face falls. "Have you seen another one?"

"I think one tried to break into my room last night."

The cherub's gaze flicks between us both, as if she's following our conversation.

He swallows. "But could it have been something else? Perhaps an owl? Or an eagle?"

"I'm sure it was the same creature, Raphael," I say. "I could smell it from inside my room, through my window. And I know it sounds unbelievable, but it seemed to be sniffing – like a scent hound."

I tell him what happened in the night. As I describe it all, I watch him carefully. I try not to miss anything, but some of it is so difficult to describe, like a dream. Talking about it brings the fear rushing back and I find myself shaking.

I look up at the clear sky. My house, sandwiched between the town and the forest beyond, seems to be watching us. I wonder if Mother has noticed I've gone yet, or if she's still calling for me, waiting for someone to bring her breakfast in bed.

"Perhaps it was looking for the cherub," Raphael says.

I glance at her, praying she can't understand what we're saying. "I guess that's possible."

He rubs his forehead. "What did the book say about these birds again?"

"Not much, and not whether they prey on cherubs."

"Well, I think we need to keep her near us, and do what we can to protect her."

"She hasn't been out of my sight, Raphael, apart from when I go down to eat, but I can't take her with me then."

We sit in silence, watching the cherub.

"Anyway, who did you see in the forest?" I feel a need to change the subject.

"It was old Frau Fischer. After I'd buried the bird, I heard a noise in the distance. It didn't sound like an animal, so I followed the cries, and that's when I found her. She'd fallen in her garden. I carried her into her cottage, but thought I should stay with her for a while, and then it became too dark to walk home."

"Oh, that's terrible,' I say. "Was she badly injured?"

"No, she's bruised, but seemed very cheerful this morning. You'd never have guessed anything happened the day before. I think she liked having me there. She's probably lonely. I'm going to take her some food this morning."

"I'm coming with you," I say, terrified at the thought of him going back into the forest on his own.

"You don't need to, Cassie. I can look after myself."

"But you don't know that! There's something out there, Raphael." I glance towards the forest. I hate the thought of going back there too, but I know he'll be safer with the cherub and me. Something tells me she needs to stay close to both of us. "And anyway," I add, "Emaline always has plenty of food in the kitchen."

Raphael smiles. "Well, if you're sure you don't mind."

"I'm certain," I say.

Chapter Fourteen

The temperature plummets as we reach the forest. I shiver and pull my cloak tightly round myself. I can't help glancing up, checking for movement above, worrying this is a terrible mistake. But the forest is alive with life, not silent like last time. Owlets shriek nearby, alarmed at the sight of us passing too close to their nest. The sudden squeal of a far-off creature crashing about in the undergrowth makes me jump.

Fledgling

"What was that?" I say.

"It sounds like a boar," Raphael says, glancing around.

I nod, remembering it's mating season.

The cherub is wobbling about in my basket, clutching the rim with cold-looking fingers. She looks around with wide eyes, taking everything in. She's making a strange clicking sound and I glance down at her. She smiles up at me and clicks again, her eyes sparkling.

"Are you talking to me?" I laugh, relieved she isn't growling like the last time we were here, but she falls silent as something catches her attention in the distance. I pull a tea towel over her head to hide her from anything that might be watching us, but she shakes it off and frowns at me.

A gust of wind whips through the trees, flicking at leaves, causing branches to rise and fall like waves. The breeze catches my hair, tugging it away from my face. Raphael turns to smile at me, and I smile back.

We venture deeper into the forest, our feet crunching through fallen leaves, rotting branches collapsing under our boots. I look about, searching the trees for any sign of movement.

Two pairs of unblinking yellow eyes stare at us from a hollow in an old oak. My heart misses a beat, but then I realise it's just a pair of owls – perhaps the protective parents of the owlets I heard earlier. I'm surprised to see them awake at this time of day.

Despite the warmth from my thick cloak, I shudder. Raphael, in his rolled-up shirtsleeves, seems oblivious to the cold.

"How far now?" I say.

"Not much further. We should be there soon."

I wonder how he remembers the way to Frau Fischer's cottage. Everything in this dense part of the forest looks the same and there are few landmarks to guide the way. I rarely venture past the little clearing where I was attacked, so heading deeper into the forest should terrify me. But with the cherub tucked up alongside Frau Fischer's food in my basket and Raphael by my side, I start to feel strangely safe.

We reach a clearing on high ground, and from here, through a narrow gap in the trees, I spot the Bahl, the long ridge that runs the length of the north-eastern edge of the forest. The sun lights up the ancient walls of Wenningstein Castle, long since abandoned and isolated from the rest of the world on the ridge's highest point. As I stop to look at it, a large bird flies out of one of its empty windows.

"Can I carry her for a while?" Raphael says, nodding towards the cherub.

"Of course," I say, "but be careful not to let her go."

I hold my basket up to Raphael and he lifts her out. She flutters up into his arms so enthusiastically he staggers backwards, surprised by her speed and weight. She grabs hold of his shirt and clings to him like a limpet, bunching the white cotton tightly in her fingers. She flutters her wings like a hummingbird and tucks her little toes into his belt for support. He wraps his arms round her. She looks so tiny next to him.

"Do you think we'll be able to persuade Frau Fischer to come back with us, if she needs looking after?" I say, finally drawing my eyes away from them both.

Raphael steps ahead of me and holds a slender branch back as he waits for me to pass. "I think she'd rather die out here alone than come back to the town."

"Surely she'd want someone to help her? Maybe she should be in the sanatorium."

Raphael hesitates as if deciding whether to tell me something. "I think she had a bad experience in Edenburg a long time ago. I don't know what it was, but she says she'll never go back to the town, however ill she gets."

"She sounds like Grandma."

He nods. "But it's more than stubbornness. I think she's afraid of something. But she's looking after herself quite well, despite everything. She says she lives off the milk from her goat and the bread she bakes on her stove." He turns to face me and smiles. "We could bring the nurses out here to see her, if she won't come back with us."

I laugh at the thought of Crunch and Grind crashing through the forest like a pair of wild boars. "I can't see them wanting to come out this far," I say, and Raphael grins.

Narrow branches flick at our faces as we ease our way past trees growing so close together that we struggle to squeeze through.

We eventually reach a clearing with a ramshackle wooden cottage in the middle. The house is tiny – an old hunting lodge with a small door, two windows and a chimney. A narrow path leads up to the door. It's quite overgrown, but I can just make out a row of round white stones carefully placed up each side of the path, suggesting the garden was once well tended. Apart from a scruffy goat tethered to a stake to the side of the house, there is no sign of life. I take the cherub from Raphael and place her back in the basket.

We reach the front door and I knock gently. When there is no reply I turn the handle and push the door open. It takes a moment for my eyes to adjust to the gloom inside.

"Hello, Frau Fischer!" Raphael calls out from behind me. "It's me, Raphael. I've brought my friend Cassie to see you."

The room is cold and has the feeling of somewhere that hasn't been lived in for a long time. A stack of hay bales has been arranged by the window for seating. The only shelf in the room is piled high with a plethora of strange-looking items: a small animal skull, an assortment of rusting hunting knives and some colourful glass bottles. A cobweb-covered log pile leans next to the unlit stove. I rub my arms. It's colder in here than outside. I can't believe Frau Fischer has baked any bread for a long time.

A string of bratwurst and dry herbs hang from a low beam. Despite the age and neglect, the room doesn't smell unpleasant – just of sage and blood sausage and straw.

It is among all this that I spot her – the tiniest, frailest woman I have ever seen. She is so small she looks like a child, and is so well hidden in her rocking chair under a pile of old blankets that I almost miss her. She looks up at us through watery eyes.

"Raphael?" she cries. "My boy! You've come again!" She claps her hands together in glee.

Raphael grins at her. "We wanted to check you were

well, Frau Fischer. After your fall. And we've brought you some food. How are you feeling today?"

"Oh, I am just fine, mein Schatz. Just an odd bruise here and there." Her right hand is dark blue, suggesting it's taken a terrible blow. She grins at Raphael. "I don't see anyone for years and then you turn up, and then you come again with your Freundin!" She winks at Raphael and, even in this light, I'm certain I see him blushing.

"Do you have many visitors, Frau Fischer?" I say, perching on a wobbly milking stool near the unlit stove. I can't believe anyone would even know she was here, so far from Edenburg.

She crosses her arms and makes a harrumphing sound. "Only *those birds*," she says, jerking her head towards the ceiling.

"Birds?" I say, my heart skipping a beat.

"And my boy."

"You have a son?" I say.

"No, of course I don't have a son! *He's* the nearest I've got to my own boy." She nods towards Raphael.

"That's nice of you to say," Raphael says, taking her hands in his. "But we only met yesterday."

She winks at him and chuckles.

"And the birds?" I say, glancing at Raphael. "Were there many of them?"

"Yes, the sky was full of them. Noisy beasts. All over my roof like they owned the place, they were, flapping about with their big wings and stinking breath. Made it so dark in here I could barely see beyond the end of my nose!"

Raphael pulls back the dusty curtain and peers outside.

"Did they try to hurt you?" I say.

"No, dear," she says, examining her hand. "This was from the fall, nothing to do with them. But they frightened Olga, my old goat, out of her senses."

She turns to Raphael, and smiles at him with a toothless grin. "Ah, you're a good boy. I knew you'd come back." She stares at him for a while, scrutinising him. "I'd never forget those eyes. Blue as periwinkles. Haven't changed since you was a newborn. Never seen eyes like them."

There *is* something strangely hypnotic about Raphael's eyes, but I'm too astonished by what she's just said to say anything about that. "Did you know him when he was a baby?" I say.

"Know him? I found him! Not that anyone ever said thank you. Some days I wish I'd never bothered. Should have raised him meself. Could have done with a big strong boy about the house." She pinches one of Raphael's arms and winks at him again.

"I think you might have confused me with someone else, Frau Fischer," he says, smiling awkwardly. "I was born in Edenburg."

She laughs until she coughs, a horrible hack that makes her eyes water. She shouldn't be alone here in this cold, damp cottage.

"They took him from me," she says, still wheezing, clutching her chest as if in pain. "Them big shots in the Rathaus. Didn't think I'd be a good mama. Just took him away, they did. No pleases or thank-yous. Just off you go, Frau Fischer, back to the forest. Don't bother to come and visit the baby." She waggles a bony finger at Raphael. "You was all theirs, from the moment they set their beady eyes on you."

Raphael runs his fingers through his hair. "I don't know about any of this," he says, looking at me desperately, as if hoping I'll be able to say something to help.

Is it possible she isn't as mad as she sounds? Might she really have found him in the forest? I've heard stories of that sort of thing happening, of people abandoning their babies when they can't look after them themselves.

She beams at Raphael. "Ooh, those eyes!" she says. "As bright as the day you arrived!"

"Arrived? What do you mean, Frau Fischer?" I try not to sound impatient. "I thought you said you *found* him." I glance at the cherub, praying she'll keep quiet. Still half concealed in the basket, I can tell she's listening to our conversation. "Do you mean when he came to see you yesterday?"

"No, dear." She speaks slowly to me as if I'm stupid. "I mean when he was brought here when he was just a babe. Like I said."

I start to wonder if she has been at the Apfelwein. But she doesn't smell drunk.

"What do you mean, *brought here when I was just a babe*?" Raphael says.

"When the angels brought you down, dear."

"I think you must have made a mistake," I say, my voice sounding too brittle. "Raphael was definitely born in Edenburg." I look at him. "You were born in Edenburg, weren't you, Raphael?"

Raphael looks ashen. He sits on one of the hay bales and puts his hands over his face.

She must have bumped her head when she fell yesterday. But then the cherub was blown into my room. People say cherubs don't exist, but she is here with me now in my basket, looking up at me. This is different, though. Raphael is just a boy. Not quite like the other boys in the town, but no one in their right mind could believe he was delivered to Earth by angels.

Raphael gets up and edges towards the door, and I'm suddenly desperate to get out of here too. Away from this dank air and back into the forest. Even the prospect of home seems enticing.

I reach into my basket. "Here's some bread, Frau Fischer, enough to last for a couple of days. And a sausage. My maid Emaline made it. It tastes better than it looks." I find a plate on the floor near her rocking chair, wipe it on my dress, place the sausage on it and pass it to her.

She peers closely at the fat sausage. "They lit up the whole forest, they did. Like giant fireflies. Bigger than any person I've ever seen. Came down through the trees. Two of them, there were. Turned everything white, like it was snowing." She looks out at the sky and her eyes shine. "I was just out milking the goat, minding my own business. Not Olga, mind. It was before her time. It was Agatha then – I think." She picks up the sausage, sniffs it and puts it back down again. "Or was it Hette?" I edge towards the door. I don't want to hear any more of this. "She was a good little milker, Hette. Best cheese in Bavaria from her milk, people said. Used to sell it at the market. Before they took my boy." She puckers her lips crossly.

She definitely isn't drunk. A bit confused, perhaps,

but not drunk.

She looks from me to Raphael, as if realising we don't believe her. "They *was* angels. I'm not making it up. I know it doesn't sound right, but it's how it happened. Huge, they were, with wings from head to toe."

"And they brought *him*?" I whisper, looking at Raphael.

"Yes, they brought *him*," she says, waggling a finger at Raphael. "Left him in an owls' nest in a tree trunk."

"We need to go, Cassie," Raphael says abruptly. "I have to get home. We'll send Crunch and Grind out to see you, Frau Fischer. To check you over." He stumbles towards the door.

I open my mouth to say something, but, seeing the expression on Raphael's face, I stop myself. Surely he can't believe this!

"No, you won't," Frau Fischer says. "If you send those two over, I shan't let them in."

I grab the cherub and the basket and follow Raphael outside, mumbling a farewell to Frau Fischer as I close the door behind us. "She's just an old lady," I say, trotting down the path behind him. "She's just imagining things."

Raphael turns to me. His face is flushed. "Maybe she isn't imagining it," he says, before heading into the darkness of the forest. I run behind him, struggling to keep up.

"She spends too long on her own, Raphael. People like that make up stories sometimes. *She* probably believes it's true." The cherub leaps up from the basket into my arms. I hold her on my hip and quickly wrap my shawl round her, glancing up again into the treetops. I wonder if I could protect her if we are attacked again. "You don't believe her, do you?"

He doesn't reply, but stops suddenly and swings round to face me. His face is wet with tears.

"I don't want to believe it," he cries. "But…"

"But what, Raphael?"

"I don't know. It's just…"

I reach out towards him, but he shakes his head and staggers away from me. "Don't, please," he says.

I sob. "Raphael! Please talk to me! I want to help you."

Raphael looks at me with such intensity I feel as if the breath is being drawn from my lungs. He sighs. "I've been having dreams," he says quietly. "I thought I was going mad." He looks above me, at the treetops. "Oh, I don't know." He seems to be trying to shake a thought from his head, "I didn't get much sleep last night. I'm too tired to think straight."

"What dreams?" I say.

"Well, something strangely like what Frau Fischer described," he says, still staring into the trees as if something has caught his eye. "Which is why I can't say she's lying – I need to get back, Cassie. I promised Papa I'd check on the shop."

I nod, not trusting myself to speak. We walk together, side by side, in silence until the trees thin and Edenburg comes into view. I chew on my lip, wishing I'd asked Frau Fischer more about the birds that had been tormenting her. If she's telling the truth about Raphael, maybe that was true too, and there are more of them out here. Raphael places his hand briefly on the cherub's head and smiles at me before turning away and heading off towards his cottage. I stand and watch his retreating back, praying he will turn and wave goodbye, but he doesn't.

I run home, conscious of the cherub watching me from under my shawl. Frau Fischer's words about Raphael and the angels are still swirling about my mind. If she is telling the truth, then who, or what, is Raphael? And where did he really come from?

Chapter Fifteen

I creep into the house, unable to forget the expression on Raphael's face as he left me.

The cherub flutters up from the basket and settles on my shoulder. I lift her up and plonk her back into the basket, but she flies straight back to my shoulder. Mother is making a strange noise up in the music room. She's singing one very long high note followed by a slightly different but equally high note. Just as I reach the safety of my bedroom, a sudden noise behind me makes me jump.

"Boo!"

I spin round, heart pounding, fists balled, and come face to face with Papa. The cherub watches him quietly from my shoulder. He looks like he's in a good mood.

"Just the person I'm looking for," he says, grinning.

I am speechless for a second and glance at the cherub – but he doesn't appear to notice her. I wonder if he is in need of new spectacles.

"Hello, Papa," I say cautiously, not wanting to startle the cherub. "You shouldn't jump out at me like that."

"Sorry, darling," he says, laughing. "I couldn't help myself; it was too good an opportunity." His face is inches from mine. "Are you all right? You look like you've seen a ghost."

I glance at him and then at the cherub again. "I am well, thank you," I reply, my voice too shrill.

"Ah, good, you're looking rather peaky," he says. "Too pale, like your mother. What you need is some fresh air."

He shuffles away towards his bedroom, before turning back to me again, a hand raised, as if suddenly remembering what he wanted. "Actually, I do have a favour to ask." He nods his head towards Mother's music room. "Your mother is behaving a little strangely.

Would you be a dear?"

"Would I be a dear and what?" I say, wondering again at what point he will notice the cherub perched on my shoulder.

"I've tried talking to her, but she got rather cross with me." He grimaces extravagantly. "I know it's a terrible bore, but would you pop up and have a word? Find out what she's up to, eh?"

The cherub buzzes her wings, lifts up into the air, and flies towards Papa. Slowly, she circles his head, examining him like a specimen in a museum. She seems invisible to him. But I can see her, and so can Raphael, so how can Papa not?

"All right," I say, grumbling under my breath.

I run to my room, squeeze the cherub into the boot box and close the door carefully before heading up to see Mother.

★

I find her kneeling in the centre of the room, facing a tall thin plant stand with a crystal glass perched on top. The plant that normally lives on the stand has been thrown across the room and now lies in a heap of broken terracotta under one of the windows. Wet-looking soil is splattered up the wall.

Dressed in a low-cut red gown with her usual cape,

Mother is breathing in and out deeply, her chest rising and falling with each breath. Her eyes are closed. She is singing a single high note again, and I stand awkwardly and wait until she stops to take another breath.

"Mother?"

She opens her eyes and waves me away. "Leave, Cassie. Can you not see I am busy?"

"But we were worried about you, and wondered what you were doing."

She closes her eyes and exhales slowly through pursed lips. After a deep intake of breath, she resumes the long piercing note again, her crimson lips almost touching the glass. A shadow falls across the room and I glance nervously outside. I pull my shawl more tightly round my shoulders. Does Mother not feel the cold? I touch the radiator. It is like ice.

Why hasn't Emaline lit the fire if the heating isn't working properly up here? Maybe Mother wouldn't let her. She's always telling me how little money we have, and how one day we might have to survive without Emaline. Of course, we couldn't possibly survive without her, as none of us is capable of even frying a bratwurst. I can maintain the owlery and keep everything working in the engine room. But feeding ourselves? That is a different matter altogether.

Eventually Mother stops, breathes in deeply and opens her eyes to look at me.

"Are you still here?"

As she resumes her note, I scoop up pieces of broken plant pot and brush soil from the wall with the sleeve of my dress.

"Is that an F?" I say, when she draws breath again.

"It's a high C. I would have hoped, with all your musical training, you might have known that."

I look at her in surprise, wondering what she means by *musical training*. I don't think I've had a music lesson in my life, apart from being exposed to her singing every day. And I don't think Grandma's dancing lessons count.

"But why are you singing to a glass, Mother?"

"I am trying to shatter it into a thousand pieces."

I look at her incredulously. "But how would singing to it break the glass?"

"It's to do with resonant frequency, darling. The details are shockingly boring."

"Mother, please tell me," I say. "How does this resonant frequency work? Can one's voice really break a glass?"

"If it's loud enough and if one gets the note just right," she says. "Every glass has its own frequency and if I manage to match that with sufficient volume, then the glass should explode."

"And how do you know which note to sing?"

"I don't," she says. "I just have to keep trying until I find the right one."

This explains why it has been going on for so long.

"Anyway, please leave me alone now." She suddenly looks gloomy, and rubs her hands over her face.

"Does it matter if you can't shatter the glass?" I say, hoping to make her feel better. This must be important to her, but, as much as I wish otherwise, I cannot believe such a thing is possible.

She looks towards the window and sighs. It is getting dark outside. I jump up and flick the switch on the lamp in the corner of the room.

"It does if you're old and washed up like me," she says eventually.

I look at her aghast. "You're not old and washed up. You're beautiful, Mother, you know that. And you're the best soprano in Bavaria."

I remember how the *Münchener Opern Revue* had been so effusive in its praise of her. I'm sure that can't have been more than two years ago. The article had described her as bold and beautiful, a tour de force on the München opera scene.

She laughs. "You are kind, darling. But of course you

don't know what you're talking about."

"I do know that you can sing, Mother," I say, bristling slightly.

"Well, as it happens, it appears my days are numbered." She notices my shocked face. "At the opera, darling. I'm not planning on dying just yet."

"What do you mean, Mama? Do they not want you any more?"

"There are younger women snapping at my heels," she says, "and a new Generalmusikdirektor. Apparently my voice is not what it once was."

"And you're planning to astonish them with this glass-breaking trick?"

"It isn't a trick," she says. "It's how I'm going to keep this ridiculous roof over our heads." She turns to me and narrows her eyes. "And where are we with the owls?"

I shake my head. "I'm still looking into it," I say, my fingers crossed behind my back.

She rises from the floor as if lifted by an invisible thread, glides across the room and throws open a window. A gust of cold air hits her hard in the face and she turns back to me, tears streaming down her cheeks. Horrified to see her like this, I take a step towards her, but she backs away. "Go!" she says, turning away from me again. I back out of the room, and run downstairs, swallowing hard to fight away my own tears.

I've never seen Mother like this, and wish I knew what to do to make her feel better. I cannot imagine her not being an opera singer. It is all she has ever been.

Chapter Sixteen

Shaking away thoughts of Mother for now, I decide to go and speak to Emaline about Frau Fischer. I find her in the kitchen, preparing dinner.

"Hello, Emaline," I say, contemplating the best way to broach the subject. She is sitting at the table, rolling out pastry. A pan is bubbling on the range.

"Ooh, what's for supper?" I say, leaning over the pan, inhaling the steam. "It smells delicious."

"Rabbit pie," she says. "And apple strudel. What *she* wanted."

I can't remember what Mother had requested, but nod anyway. "I'm sure that will be perfect. Where did the rabbit come from?"

"Fresh from the forest. A young 'un. Should be nice and tender."

I shudder at the thought. I know the forest is full of traps, and it's how people feed themselves, but the idea of a rabbit dying in a snare is too awful to contemplate. "Did *you* trap it?" I say.

She looks at me as if I'm mad. "No."

She rolls the pastry over the top of a pie dish and shuffles over to the sink to wash her hands.

"Emaline," I say.

She turns to me and sighs. "Ja?" she says, pulling a towel from a drawer to dry her hands. They're huge calloused things, presumably from all the years spent cleaning up after us.

"We bumped into someone in the forest yesterday, and I wondered what you knew about her."

She looks at me and rolls her eyes. "Frau Fischer, was it?"

"How did you know?"

"She's the only one mad enough to live out there.

It's not right."

"Do you think she is mad? I was just wondering—"
I don't know what to say next. How much should I tell
her? I think I trust her, but you can never be sure with
people.

"As hops."

"I'm sorry?"

"Mad as hops. Like I said. Should be in an asylum,
that one."

"And why do you say that?" It's an awful way to
describe someone, especially a lonely old person.

She shrugs. "Say as I see." She looks at me carefully.
"So where did you find her?"

"We went to her cottage. She'd fallen in her garden
and Raphael had heard her cries for help. He was
worried about her being on her own." I don't mention
the food I stole from the pantry.

"You went out there with Raphael?"

"Yes," I say. "He'd found her in a terrible state and
stayed all night at her cottage to look after her. I thought
she seemed sweet. A bit cross at times, but nice."

"Did she talk about *him*?"

"About who?"

"Raphael."

"Not really," I say cautiously.

She rolls her eyes. "Spread some story about him when he was a young one. Nonsense, it was. Rattlepuss, she is."

I can see people might describe her as a gossip. "What story, Emaline?"

"Something and nothing," she says, lifting the kettle from the range and pouring boiling water into the sink. She shakes whiting into the hot water, dips her scrubbing brush in and sets about attacking the kitchen table.

"Was it about her finding Raphael as a baby?"

She stops scrubbing but remains hunched over the table.

"Is that what she told you?" she says, turning round. "Did she tell you how she turned up in town, babe in arms, claiming she found him in an owls' nest? As if anyone believed that rubbish. It wasn't right. Some said she'd stolen him from travellers."

"Did anyone believe her?"

"No. And they took the babe away. Adopted by Herr Vogel and his wife."

So it is true he was adopted.

"She wouldn't leave them alone after that. They sent her packing in the end. Just wanted some peace and quiet with their new babe."

"She returned to the forest?"

121

"Ja, but not before spreading more of her rubbish."

I stand and look at Emaline for a while, not knowing what to say.

But something makes me believe Frau Fischer's version of events.

Chapter Seventeen

As I return to my room, still mulling over Emaline's words, I notice an unpleasant smell in the corridor that seems to be coming from the old leather trunk. It must be my cape, but I can't believe the stench has intensified so much in just a day. Holding my breath, I open the lid and reach inside. It's bloodier than I remember it being. Swearing under my breath, I pull it out and drop it to the floor. I'll have to throw it in the boiler after all.

As I close the lid I notice a small framed painting tucked behind the broken parasol. I pull it out to look at it. It is old and faded, but recognisable as a portrait of a boy. He looks about fourteen and is dressed strangely in breeches, knee-length leather boots and an embroidered shirt. His hair falls to his shoulders in blond curls. There is elaborate writing at the bottom of the picture. It is the name of the boy and a date.

Ramiel Engel.

1824.

But he looks exactly like Raphael! I take the picture to the window and examine it carefully. The boy in this picture could be Raphael's twin.

I push it into my pocket and, holding the cape between my thumb and forefinger, I run to the zip, dragging the cape behind me. I jump on to the platform and shoot down through the house. Reaching the engine room, I crank open the boiler door, hurl the cape in and watch with a lump in my throat as it is engulfed in flames.

I pull the picture out of my pocket and look at it again. The boy's hair is longer than Raphael's, and of course it is difficult to judge his height from a picture like this, but he has the same build, the same stance and the same direct gaze. Despite the picture being so faded, I can see the boy's eyes are a startling shade of blue. Grandma might know about this. She used to love talking about our ancestors when she was still well. She will know who he is.

★

Grandma smiles as I walk into her room. "Hello, darling," she whispers.

I lean over and kiss her forehead. "Hello, Grandma," I say. "I thought I'd come to see how you are." I pull a chair from the corner of the room and sit next to the bed. "Have you had anything to eat today?" I raise my voice as her hearing isn't what it once was.

"Yes, thank you. Dear Emaline brought me some delicious mushroom soup earlier. I feel quite perked up by it."

I smile at her, relieved the soup helped. But she doesn't look at all perky to me, with her hollow cheeks and sharp bones jutting through her sheets. "Would you like some water? Or something stronger?" I say, touching her hand gently.

"No, dear, thank you."

We sit in silence for a while.

"Grandma?"

"Yes, darling?"

"I found a picture just now, of a boy, and I wondered who he was. It was in the trunk in the corridor, by the cabinet of curiosities. His name is written at the bottom. Ramiel Engel. Do you know who he might be?"

Grandma takes a sharp breath. Of course he would have died long before she was born, but she may have heard of him.

"Let's see," she says, tapping her fingers as if counting. "Ramiel was your great-great-grandfather's son, so that would make him your great-great-uncle."

"But I have never heard anyone talk about him, or even mention his name."

"That's probably because no one talks about him."

"Did he do something terrible?"

"No, it wasn't that."

She closes her eyes, as if wishing to end the conversation.

"What was it then, Grandma?" I feel guilty questioning her like this.

"He died, that's what it was."

"And did he have children?"

"No, dear, he died too young for that."

"Oh. How old was he? When he died, I mean?"

"He was fifteen."

I am shocked, but I know people in the past didn't live as long as they do now. Even today, with sanatoriums, and doctors who understand so much about illness, people still die young.

"Was it an illness?" I say. "Or an accident?"

"I'm not sure *exactly* what happened, but I believe it was very sudden." She looks away from me. "His parents never fully recovered, as you can imagine when something like that happens."

The morphine pump hisses and heaves and Grandma exhales deeply.

I pull the picture out of my pocket and look at it.

"Do you know what year he died, Grandma?"

She thinks for a minute. "I believe it was probably somewhere around the year 1824."

So the portrait was painted the year he died.

"Can I see it?"

"Of course." I find Grandma's pince-nez on her bedside table and perch them on her face. She peers through them at the picture, her nose almost touching the old canvas.

"But that's Raphael," she says. "That can't be right."

"It does look like him," I say. "But look at the date on the bottom. It says 1824. And look at his clothes. Raphael would never wear anything like that."

"I have never seen a painting of Ramiel," Grandma says, looking confused.

I hear a noise from somewhere in the house. A short

cry, followed by silence.

"I need to go, Grandma," I say, my heart skipping a beat. "I'll come and see you later when you've had a rest."

"Thank you, darling, that would be lovely," she says, tapping my hand gently with her fingertips.

As I leave, she calls out after me. "Of course, Ramiel was adopted. He was never quite like the rest of them."

I hear another shriek, as Grandma's words race around my head. Ramiel was adopted. Like Raphael.

But any thoughts about Ramiel disappear as soon as I reach my room.

Chapter Eighteen

My bedroom door is ajar. I know I closed it properly.

I push it open slowly.

The first thing I see is Bram crouching on the floor next to my wardrobe, staring up with wide frightened eyes and flattened ears.

The cherub is perched on the little display shelf over my bed, her feet dangling over the edge, wings open as if about to take flight. Her eyes are as dark as coal.

Bram is watching her.

And she is watching Bram.

"Bram, come here," I whisper, creeping towards him with outstretched arms. He looks at me with irritation and growls. I scoop him up but he wriggles from my grip and lands with a thump back on the floor. He lowers himself until his round belly is just a fraction of an inch from the floorboards and flicks his tail from side to side. He makes the strangest sound. It is a deep, decidedly uncatlike wail. I close my door carefully behind me. This would not be a good moment for Papa to poke his head in.

The cherub's head is tilted slightly to one side and a smile flickers across her lips, almost as if she is goading Bram into attacking her.

I silently plead with Bram not to do anything stupid, but before I can stop him, and with lightning speed, he leaps up towards the cherub.

I scream, but it's too late. Bram is already mid-flight and I can't reach him in time. He is two feet up in the air and halfway across the room when something seems to block his path. It's almost as if he has hit a rubber wall, and he bounces back across the room and lands heavily in front of the wardrobe. He shakes himself down and flattens his ears. He tries again, but exactly the same thing happens. He wails in frustration.

I step towards the cherub cautiously, my arms in front of me, tapping the air as if blindfolded. Halfway across the room my fingertips meet resistance. I push gently and feel something soft and spongy. The cherub watches me, eyebrows raised. As I run my fingers along the invisible jelly-like wall I realise that it spans the width of my room.

I prod it, harder this time, and with a soft pop, my fingers penetrate the strange mass. When my hand is fully immersed, pressure builds around it as if it is being squeezed by an unseen force. I push in further until my whole arm is buried, and again, the pressure wraps round my arm like a tourniquet. I retract it quickly with another pop and the sensation subsides.

Intrigued more than frightened, I push my whole body against the invisible wall. With a sucking sound it draws me in and I find myself surrounded by a luminescence of blue – of swirling lights and distant noise, as if someone far away is humming a lullaby. I try to speak, but my mouth is heavy and awkward, and what noise I am able to make sounds muffled. My breathing is laboured and my chest burns as if I am inhaling fire. This is what I felt the night the Sturmfalke tried to break in.

Light-headed now and unable to bear it any longer,

I fight my way out. As the luminescence releases me, I catch sight of my reflection in the wardrobe mirror. I look dishevelled, and as I run my hands through my hair, my fingers fizz. I look like I have had an electric shock.

Bram is pressed up against the door, hackles raised. He miaows urgently, shouting at me to let him out. I open the door and he skitters away down the corridor.

The cherub must have been protecting herself from Bram with some sort of invisible barrier. She wouldn't let him get close to her, but she chose to let *me* in. Was this some sort of warning for him to stay away? Or did she wish to show me how she can protect me?

I sit on my bed and hold my arms out. She whirrs her wings, flies down to me and lands heavily on my knee, looking quite pleased with herself. I wrap my arms round her and breathe her in. "That was mean," I say. "You mustn't hurt Bram. And he can be vicious! He might have hurt *you*!"

She looks at me and almost laughs.

Might Raphael be able to explain this? He seems to understand some things better than other people, despite claiming to have learned little at school.

This has given me the perfect excuse to visit.

But then the grandfather clock chimes. It's eight

o'clock. Dinner time. It will have to wait until the morning. The cherub watches me carefully, her eyes bright and full of light. They are sparkling.

"Would you like to come with me to see Raphael tomorrow?" I say.

She purrs in my ear. Of course she would. I carry her across the room and we look out.

Raphael's window is wide open. He must be home.

Chapter Nineteen

I arrive early at Raphael's house and peer in through the kitchen window. The room is empty. Stepping back across the lane I crane my neck to get a better view of his bedroom window above. It is still open, as it was last night.

"Raphael, it's me. Are you up there?" I hiss.

He does not reply. I pick up a pebble and throw it at the window. It hits the glass with a clatter, before tumbling back down again. The cherub flutters from the basket and lands on my shoulder. I knock on the door, stomping my feet on the icy ground as I wait for a reply.

I knock again. When there is no response, I turn the handle, and am surprised when the door swings open. Glancing back down the lane to check no one is watching, I step inside. I have never been in Raphael's house before.

The kitchen is untidy and dominated by an old table piled high with tools. A hammer, a chisel and a little hatchet lie next to a half-eaten loaf and a slab of Butterkäse. A tin of grease sits lidless by a jug of milk. I pick the milk up and sniff it cautiously. It smells sour and has formed a skin. I place it back on the table. Raphael's mother died when he was young and Herr Vogel works long hours in the shop. I know they don't have a maid to help with these things.

I hear a noise from the floor above. It's just a small thud, but it's enough for me to know I am not alone in the house.

I call up the stairs. "Raphael, it's me, Cassie. Can I come up?"

There is no reply.

I race up the stairs, two at a time. Reaching the landing I stop and listen, but all I can hear is the crashing of my heart. The cherub grips my shoulder, her bright eyes, like mine, searching the gloom. Her breath is hot and heavy on my neck, and in the quiet our hearts beat as one. She makes a clicking sound that reminds me of the dits and dahs of my Morse code machine.

It is darker up here than downstairs. I can just make out three closed doors, and I'm not sure which will lead to Raphael's room. I open the first door and find a small tidy room with a single bed, a wardrobe and a wooden chair with a pair of overalls hanging over the back. This must be Herr Vogel's room. The next door leads into an even smaller room that smells of leather. Boxes are piled high on shelves, suggesting it is some sort of storeroom.

I open the third door.

"Raphael!" I cry, dropping my basket.

He is curled up in bed on his side, gripping his knees, his knuckles sharp and white.

"Raphael, what's happened?" I say, running to him and falling to my knees by his side. He's drenched with sweat and seems unable to speak. I take his hands in mine. They are hot and clammy and, as if realising this, he pulls them away. He smells strangely metallic, like the engine room at home.

I grab a cloth from my basket and press it to his forehead. He groans under my touch.

"Help me, Cassie," he pleads.

I search his body for sign of an accident, yet I can't see any obvious injury.

"Raphael," I say, "what have you done?"

He shakes his head. "I don't know."

"Where is your pain?"

"It's in my back."

I lean across him, and notice two small lumps visible through his sweat-soaked shirt, just over his shoulder blades. I touch one of the lumps and press down gently.

Raphael screams and I snatch my hands away. "I'm sorry!" I cry.

"Please don't touch me," he whispers.

I fight back tears. "I'm sorry," I say again. "Did you fall down the stairs?" It's the only explanation I can think of.

"No!" he cries. "This pain came from nowhere." He bites down on his lip. "It woke me this morning."

He turns to the cherub. "Please help me," he says. "I know you can."

She settles next to him on the bed, and looks at him intently.

She beats her wings and rises from the bed. Raphael uncurls, as if in a trance, and stands up, his eyes remaining locked on hers. He breathes in and out slowly, as if discovering how to do so for the first time.

The cherub flies to the centre of the room. Raphael follows her and sinks to his knees. She stands facing him on her tiptoes, her eyes ablaze.

She turns to me and beckons. I join them and they take my shaking hands in theirs. The three of us form a small circle. She closes her eyes and hums.

The air around us changes. It becomes warmer – and softer somehow. It is different to what happened in my room yesterday with Bram. Now it feels as if we are being wrapped in a cocoon of silk. My body becomes weightless. I am floating! We are just an inch or so from the floor, but Raphael and I are floating!

As we are swallowed in light and warmth, my fear leaves me. A strange aroma fills the room. It is the smell of Christmas – of pine cones and cloves, and almonds.

We rise further from the floor and I glance down nervously, frightened I might suddenly fall. Raphael is now lit up from the inside, like the cherub on the night of the attack. His veins glow through his skin, pulsating as blood pumps around his body, from his heart to his fingertips, and back to his heart again. This translucence lasts just a few seconds before the light within him fades.

The cherub remains focused entirely on him. Her

eyes flash in an explosion of colour and light.

We sink to the floor. Raphael slumps, and I reach out to hold him. His head falls on my shoulder. His body is so heavy I can barely support him. We stay like this for some time, the cherub watching us quietly. He weeps and I wrap my arms round him, needing to comfort him. As I touch his back, he gasps in pain, and warm liquid oozes between my fingers.

I quickly pull my hands away. My fingers are covered in blood.

He looks at my hands. "Is that from my back?"

I nod.

"Can you bear to look? I would do it myself – if I could."

I nod, and lean over his shoulder. The back of his shirt is now drenched in blood.

"I'll have to take your shirt off. To see what's happening. Do you mind?"

He shakes his head and I undo the buttons running down the front of his shirt. I push it back over his shoulders, easing his arms, one at a time, through each sleeve, but his congealing blood has glued it to his back. I carefully peel it away from his body, and he gasps at each tiny movement. Nausea rises in my throat. I take a deep breath and swallow hard.

The cherub closes her eyes and sinks into a deep trance.

Raphael cries out each time I tug at his shirt. "I'm so sorry," I say again and again.

"It's not your fault," he whispers.

I notice a small cup next to his bed. I jump up, grab it and pour a little water down his back. I slowly separate his shirt from his back and reveal two long wounds running down from his shoulder blades.

His back has been torn open in two places.

Blood is trickling down his spine and pooling on the floor.

"What can you see?" he says.

I have never seen anything like it.

This has happened since I have been here.

"Please, Cassie – you must tell me what you can see."

"I'm not sure," I say, praying I sound calmer than I feel. "I just need to clean the wounds first."

I rush downstairs and into the garden, find the water pump at the side of the house, and quickly fill a clean-looking metal bucket. It will have to do. I inhale a lungful of fresh air before returning to Raphael's room.

He is just as I left him. I pull the sheet from his bed, tear a strip from it, dip it into the icy water and press it against his wounds. Something white is protruding through one of them. I am certain it isn't bone, but with all the blood, it is difficult to tell what it is. I don't know if I'm doing the right thing, but I do know I should clean the wounds to prevent infection. I press against his back to stem the bleeding, and as I do so I feel a small movement under my fingers.

I jump back and scream.

Something from inside the wound flicks out. But whatever it is remains attached to Raphael's body. I examine it carefully, my heart pounding.

"What's happening, Cassie?" he cries. "I can feel something moving in my back!"

"I'm just trying to work out what it is," I say, relieved he cannot see my face. I run to the window and lean out, breathing in the cold mountain air.

A foul metallic stench hangs in the room. The cherub sits, head bowed, eyes closed, as if she is praying. Raphael crawls to her side.

He looks up at me through bloodshot eyes. "Please tell me, Cassie."

I gently touch the sharp narrow lump that is now sticking out.

I gasp before I can stop myself.

"What is it? What can you see? Can you see feathers?"

"Yes," I say quietly. "Yes. I can see feathers."

"I knew it," he says, tears rolling down his face. "I knew this must be it. This is what has been happening in my dreams. Every time I close my eyes to sleep, this is what I see." He looks up at me through streaming eyes. "I thought I was losing my mind. But I don't want this. I don't want to be like this, Cassie!"

The cherub rouses and begins to sing. It is the strangest sound I have ever heard. Beginning as one shrill note, it fills the room before taking on a physical form. I can *see* it! I can *see* the cherub's song. It gathers about Raphael, swirling around him like a dancer in silks, enveloping him in its soft embrace.

He rises from the floor. His face is peaceful now, and it seems his pain and fear are gone. He looks at me through deep blue eyes.

The room swims and my mind dances with terrifying thoughts. Frau Fischer's face flickers inches from mine. She laughs, spittle running down her chin. "I told you he was delivered by angels. You all said I was a liar. *Seeing things*, you said. Thought I was mad! But now you know I'm not!"

Suddenly I am consumed with a rage I have never felt before.

"Did you do this?" I shout at the cherub. "Have you done this to him? Why couldn't you leave him alone?"

I am shaken by the anger in my voice. "Is that why you are here? To turn Raphael into some sort of—" I stop myself. "What have you turned him into? One of you?"

She reaches her arms out towards me, but I turn away. I curl up in a ball, sobbing so hard my chest aches.

After some time, I realise I am crying for myself, not Raphael. I glance up. He is watching me.

"Cassie," he says. "It wasn't her. This was always going to happen."

"How was this *always* going to happen?" I say. "People don't just turn into angels."

"This is what I was born to be. I prayed I could be like everyone else. A normal boy. That's all I ever wanted. But the cherub isn't here to hurt me. She's here to help. To make it easier for me."

"And you know all this from your dreams?" I whisper.

He runs his hands through his hair. "I've been having these dreams for as long as I can remember. I've tried to ignore them, hoping they'd go away. But they keep coming, Cassie! And when she arrived, I knew it was time. But I didn't think it would be quite like this."

"So this is how you knew so much about angels," I say, barely able to meet his gaze.

He nods. "But, even then, I didn't really know if I was imagining it all. And then we read about those creatures, and you were attacked in the forest—"

We sit in silence for a moment, absorbing the enormity of what is happening to him.

"I'm going to need your help," he says eventually. "I think this is just the beginning. I think there will be more times like this, and more pain, until my wings have fully grown. I'm going to need you. And the cherub. Will you help me?"

"But, how can *I* help you?" I cry.

"Can you help conceal my wings? Nobody must know about this."

I nod, ashamed to be still sobbing.

His wounds have stopped bleeding. More feathers have emerged, but they are nothing like wings; they are more like a soft, sticky down.

"They're not actually wings, Raphael," I say, hoping to reassure him. "Just some small feathers."

"The wings will come," he says.

My heart sinks. "Will it hurt like that again?"

"I don't know. But I guess that's why she had to be here with me."

The cherub flutters up from the floor and perches on the bed. I thought the decision to come and see Raphael had been mine.

"If we wrap something round you, no one will be able

to see what has happened," I say, trying to pull myself together.

I use Raphael's sheet to make a bandage and wrap it round him, before helping him into an old shirt from his wardrobe.

I turn to the cherub. "Please forgive me," I cry. "I don't know what I was saying."

She smiles at me and clacks her tongue like earlier on the landing. She repeats the noise, and I realise there is a pattern to it.

She is trying to communicate!

"She's trying to talk to us in Morse code!" I say. "Do you have a pencil?"

He nods. "Over there."

I run to his desk, snatch up his pencil, and sit down to convert the dits and dahs into letters, to work out what she is trying to tell us.

Make Raphael safe.

She makes the clicking sound again.

Raphael home. Rock house.

"Yes, yes," I say. Of course I cannot leave him here alone. I have to take him home.

"She says you need to come home with me," I say. "Maybe we can borrow Grandma's morphine, to help with the pain. If it happens again…"

I think about the angels in the books in the library. Their wings are the length of their bodies. They are vast and nothing like the scruffy little features protruding from Raphael's back. Is it possible his could grow to be like those?

I pick the cherub up and place her in my basket.

"You don't need to hide her," Raphael says.

"Of course I do," I say, tucking a cloth over her. "It would be terrible if Mother saw her."

"No, you really don't," Raphael says. "No one else can see her."

I remember how Papa seemed oblivious to her. "But how can *I* see her?" I say.

"Because she is allowing you to see her, and because she needs you," he replies. "We both do."

Chapter Twenty

Back at my house, we head straight for the library. As we pass through the owlery I notice that something has changed again. The owls are now all facing the eagle owl in the middle of the room.

"I think someone's playing tricks on me," I say, looking around.

Raphael looks at me blankly.

"The owls have moved again," I say.

"Maybe you're imagining it," he says. "You're probably feeling jumpy with everything going on."

"Probably," I say, but I know I'm not.

When we are safely inside the library I pull the door closed behind us and am immediately comforted by the familiar smell of pipe smoke and ancient leather. For a second I let myself believe my great-great-grandfather is with us, perhaps standing at the little window with a pipe balanced on his bottom lip, keeping an eye on us.

"Do you mind if I sit down? I'm not feeling too well," Raphael says, sinking into the desk chair. He flops forward and rests his head on his arms.

"Are they still hurting?" I say, noticing how his shoulder blades are jutting out sharply, despite my tight bindings.

"It's just a dull ache now," he says. "I'm sure I'll feel better after a rest." The cherub lands on the desk and assumes a cross-legged position. She watches Raphael carefully, her head on one side.

"I'll dig out the book," I say. "There might be something in there about boys turning into angels. You try to sleep."

I find the book easily and settle into the battered leather armchair under the window with it open on my lap. I turn the heavy pages impatiently, but find nothing useful.

I sense Raphael's eyes burning into the top of my head. "You need to sleep!" I say. "I'll wake you if I find anything."

"I think I'd rather stay awake."

"But you have to sleep at some point, Raphael!"

"I'll close my eyes, to keep you happy," he says. "But sleep doesn't really help at the moment."

"Because of your dreams?"

He nods. "It's as if the moment I fall asleep, that other world fills my head – and it's a world I'd rather not see." He reaches for the cherub and pulls her into his arms. She looks at him a little crossly, but allows him to hold her.

"And what do you see?" I say hesitantly.

"Oh, I don't know. It's all such a muddle, Cassie. I hear whispered words and see strange figures, and music and movement too. I definitely see two angels each time I fall asleep, but they're so ethereal and, oh, I don't know—" He pulls the cherub in more tightly and weeps.

I want to run to him, to wrap my arms round him, to comfort him, to say something helpful, but instead I sit awkwardly in my chair, wringing my hands.

"But surely you must have a choice in all this?"

He wipes his tears away. "I don't think I do. That's the problem." He nods towards my book. "Have you found anything useful in there? Any magic spells for stopping all this?" He waves a hand towards his back.

"I don't think so," I say, turning the remaining pages to double-check.

It's getting dark. I climb out of my chair and turn on the desk lamp.

"Your house feels different," Raphael says, looking around.

I glance about the room. He's right. It does feel different, but I can't work out what it is. And then I realise that everywhere is silent. Mother isn't singing, Papa isn't snoring, and Emaline isn't crashing about in the kitchen. And the house isn't moving either. It isn't swaying, or rumbling, or groaning. As we listen to this unnatural silence, I get the strangest feeling that the house is listening too.

Just then the grandfather clock rattles into action and chimes six o'clock.

I place the book on the desk and pull a chair up next to Raphael. We flick through it again together, examining each page in detail, not daring to miss a word, desperately hoping for some sort of reference to a boy who grows wings. But there is nothing. I quickly flick past the pages with the sketches of the Sturmfalken.

It grows darker still and the temperature falls. As I blow on my hands to warm them, my breath forms a little white cloud. The cherub is watching me. Her brow is furrowed as if she too is concerned.

She begins to click again.

Dit-dit-dit-dit-dit.

I start scribbling, my hands shaking.

"What's she saying?" asks Raphael, peering over my shoulder.

I frown. "She's saying: *Storm. Prepare*," I say. "Why is she telling us about the weather?"

She begins again.

"Now she's saying *Mother*," I say. "*Mother. Mother. Mother.* Do you think she means we need to tell her what's happening to you?"

She dits and dahs again.

Imminent.

The house shudders.

I shiver. "I think you should sleep in here tonight. I could find you some bedding and make up a nest for you." I don't know why I said "nest". He's not a bird.

"I was worried you were going to lock me in the engine room," he says, smiling.

"I wouldn't do that!" I say, trying to laugh.

151

I've never wondered why Grandpa had been so insistent I learn Morse code. Is it possible he knew that one day I would need it?

Chapter Twenty-One

I leave Raphael alone to go down to dinner. It is an even more miserable affair than usual tonight. Mother sits in silence at one end of the table and Papa at the other. She glistens in a long silk gown, her red lips set in a thin straight line. She's staring into the distance, as if somewhere else in her mind. Emaline slams our plates on to the table and slops supper – some sort of stew – on to them. Papa is in one of his glooms. He's slumped over the table, looking at his food through glassy eyes, pushing it about the plate like a petulant child. The fire is unlit. I'm pleased I remembered to bring a shawl with me and pull it tightly round my shoulders.

"Will you at least try to sit straight at the dinner table?" Mother snaps.

Instinctively I sit up, before realising she is talking to Papa. He pulls himself into a more upright position, redirects his gaze from his plate to Mother, and slugs the contents of his glass in one gulp. He raises the glass. "Prost, darling!"

Mother tuts and looks away.

The door creaks open and Bram saunters in.

He struts past me, tail held high, and jumps on to Mother's knee. I wish he'd sit on me sometimes, especially when it's cold like this, but he always chooses Mother. She rubs him behind his ears and even from here I can hear him purring. I remember when I was young enough to sit on her knee and how she used to wrap her arms round me and tell me how much she loved me. I don't know what changed, or when.

After serving, Emaline stands with her back to the dresser at the end of the room, arms crossed, facing us. Waiting for her next instruction from Mother.

"Has anyone been to visit Grandma recently?"

Mother says.

"Yes, I visited her today," I say.

"And how did she seem?"

"Much the same."

"The sooner this is all over, the better for everyone," she mutters into her glass of wine.

"You cannot talk about Grandma like that!" I shout.

Mother shrugs. "I'm just saying what everyone else thinks. How would you like to be plugged into some awful contraption like that for the rest of your days?"

"Well, *I* am not thinking that," I say. "It works. It stops the pain." I am seething inside, but I don't want a confrontation. I know Grandma is old and ill, but I am not ready for her to die. But then, will I ever be? My eyes sting as I fight back tears. Mother doesn't like people crying. She shouts at Papa when *he* cries. I turn my head so she can't see my face.

We eat the rest of our meal in silence. Papa suddenly scrapes his chair back and stumbles from the room. He doesn't thank Emaline for dinner, or excuse himself, and Mother watches him in silence as he leaves.

"Can I leave the table too, Mother?" I say once his footsteps have faded into the distance.

"If you must."

155

I slip a pretzel into my napkin and slink from the room.

★

I meet Raphael back in the library. He is flicking through the illuminated manuscript again, and turns to face me.

"Do you think the Sturmfalken are here because of me?" he says.

A shiver runs down my spine. "What do you mean?"

"Well, do you think it's a coincidence that you encounter one in the forest just before I start growing wings? In my dreams there is a threat. It is dark. But, oh, I just don't know, Cassie."

"I brought you this," I say, changing the subject, handing him the pretzel. "Sorry, it's all I was able to get without anyone noticing. Everyone was in a horrible mood at dinner."

He takes it from me and turns it over in his hands. "Thank you," he says, "but I'm not very hungry."

"But you can't have eaten for a day and a night!"

"I know. I just feel I don't need to." He places it on the desk.

"Would you like Crunch and Grind to come and see you?" I say, half smiling.

"I think I'll do this without their help, thanks."

"They're going to visit Frau Fischer tomorrow," I say.

"I sent a note saying I'll join them."

"Oh, she'll be furious, Cassie!" he says. "They'll probably try to take her to the sanatorium. Should I come too, in case she makes a fuss?"

I look at him, pale and ashen and probably in pain. "No, you should stay and look after the cherub." I glance at her sitting cross-legged on the windowsill, watching us. Listening to us. She raises an eyebrow as if to suggest that it might be the other way round.

Chapter Twenty-Two

I arrive the next morning at Crunch and Grind's cottage just as they're leaving. They're in matching Tyrolean hats, ready to go and see Frau Fischer. One has a stretcher strapped to her back and the other a large brown-leather knapsack.

"Guten Morgen!" I say more cheerfully than I feel.

They harrumph at me in return. I suspect they'd rather I wasn't here.

I desperately want to tell them, anyone, about Raphael, but he has sworn me to secrecy. They probably wouldn't know what to do with him anyway. Who on earth would know what to do with a boy turning into an angel? I'm certain *that* wouldn't have been in their medical training.

They lower their hats to shield their eyes from the bright morning sun and we set off at a brisk pace along the path that leads towards the forest, one nurse behind the other, me at the back. I'm pleased to get away from the house and to breathe in some fresh mountain air.

"I hope we find her better than the last time I saw her," I say, trotting to keep up with them. "Perhaps she just needs something to eat, or someone to light the stove for her." I still feel terrible for running from her house like that, but I couldn't have let Raphael walk home on his own.

They don't reply. Their heads are low, and with their hats pulled down over their ears, I wonder if they've even heard me.

The path narrows. We hesitate as we reach the forest. I glance up briefly and take a deep breath before stepping into the gloom. I am certain nothing will attack me with Crunch and Grind by my side, but still my heart crashes like a drum.

It has snowed overnight, and a soft white layer of fresh snow is trapped high above us in the wide branches of the towering firs. I stumble clumsily on the uneven ground. Crunch and Grind charge ahead, beating a path with their walking sticks, their heavy boots smashing fallen branches to smithereens. They are well camouflaged in matching knee-length lederhosen and long thick woollen socks pulled up to their shorts. Their green-felt jackets have been patched a hundred times, but look warm and weatherproof. I wish I had something practical like that to wear, but Mother would never allow such a thing.

As they surge forward, chins low and brows furrowed, they ignore each other as much as they ignore me. I trot behind them, glancing nervously up every so often. As we reach a clearing, I am briefly distracted by the sight of snow floating silently down on us. I stop and look up, allowing the flakes to land on my upturned cheeks.

They turn and wait for me, leaning heavily on their sticks, perhaps happy for a chance to draw breath. One also glances up surreptitiously, and then at the other. I am certain I notice a flicker of a thought pass between them. Perhaps it is just impatience with me. I wipe the melted snow from my face with my sleeve and run to catch up.

"Have you got other patients to see today?" I say as I reach them.

"Ja," says one.

"Do you know where Frau Fischer lives?" I say, looking around. "It seems so different to the last time I was here."

"We know where we are going," says the other.

"Do you think she might be able to stay living in her cottage?" I say. "If Raphael and I can come out to see her? If she's feeling a little better."

"Nein," says the one who spoke first.

"But she might not agree to go to the sanatorium," I say.

"We will persuade her otherwise," says the other.

Heavy flurries of snow tumble down towards us from branches no longer able to bear their load, startling me every time they land with a thump nearby. I haven't seen any wildlife today, and wonder if the snow has sent the forest creatures scurrying into the warmth of their homes.

I wish Crunch and Grind wouldn't keep glancing up at the treetops. It makes them look as nervous as I feel, and me even more jittery.

I squint at the bulging knapsack lashed to the broad back ahead of me, wondering if it contains the tools of their trade: gruesome medical devices to frighten even the bravest huntsman. I pray they don't try to do anything terrible to Frau Fischer. I'd feel even more guilty than I do already for taking them to her.

We finally reach the clearing where Frau Fischer lives. As we approach the lonely cottage, her goat, lying on a bed of soggy-looking straw, looks up at us and bleats.

Crunch and Grind hang back as we approach the front door. I squeeze past them and knock quietly, hoping not to frighten her. As I creak it open, I call out. "Hello, Frau Fischer. It's me, Cassie. Raphael's friend."

She's almost totally hidden, like last time, under a mountain of blankets, with just her eyes and nose exposed to the chill of the room. Emaline's sausage still sits uneaten beside her. She pulls the outer blanket down a little, and peers at me over the top. "He's back! I knew he'd come back!" she exclaims. "Oh, my boy!" She looks past me, her eyes searching for Raphael.

"I'm sorry. He's not here," I say, stepping towards her. "He isn't feeling very well."

Her face crumples with disappointment. "Oh, my poor, poor boy," she says, shaking her head. "It's not right; it isn't. He needs someone to look after him properly – not that *cobbler*. How could a man like *that* look after a boy like *him*?" She nods as if formulating a plan. "Next time he comes to see me I'll rustle up a piping hot cabbage casserole for him. That'll fill him up. Too scrawny by far, that boy." She looks towards the window, as if hoping he might suddenly appear. "Ah, mein Schnucki," she whispers, almost to herself.

I smile. She must have noticed how huge Raphael is.

"But I've brought Crunch and Grind to see you," I say brightly, "to check you are well." The two nurses step quietly out of the shadows, one jiggling the heavy knapsack from her back, allowing it to fall to the floor with a clatter.

"Guten Morgen," they say, both nodding slightly, touching the peaks of their hats. "We are here to take a look at you."

"You shall do no such thing!" Frau Fischer cries, jutting her chin out and trying to pull herself up from her slumped position. Crunch or Grind leans in to examine her.

"If you come any closer," she hisses, "I shall punch you on the nose!" She bunches her fists and waves them in the nurse's direction. Birdlike and fragile beneath her blankets, sharp cheekbones jutting through threadbare skin, she doesn't look like she could throw any sort of a punch. In fact, she'd probably crumble like a twig if she tried. But I don't blame her for attempting to fend off

163

Crunch and Grind's dinner-plate hands.

I kneel in front of her and take her tiny hands in mine. "They just want to check you're well," I say, leaning in close so Crunch and Grind can't hear me. "I know they look frightening, but they won't hurt you."

She peers at me through pale porcelain eyes, and I wonder what she was like when she was younger – whether her fine white hair was once blonde, or even red, and whether she liked to dance, like Grandma. I smile at her reassuringly. She smiles back, and her face fills with creases and kindness. I think she would have made a wonderful mama, if only she'd had the chance.

"Well, so long as they're quick about it," she whispers. "Tell them I have other things to do. I can't sit here all day being prodded and poked by these two –" she raises her voice and narrows her eyes – "these two ... oxen!" She shouts the last bit to ensure Crunch and Grind hear her properly.

Ignoring her, one of the nurses moves in and sets about running a series of checks – examining her eyes through a large brass magnifying glass, recording her pulse, checking her reflexes with a little wooden hammer. All the while Frau Fischer twists away from them like a child, making their job as difficult as she can.

One of the nurses scribbles some notes into a large leather book. She glances at the other with a concerned expression, before taking Frau Fischer's pulse again.

"I am very sorry," she says eventually, "but we are going to have to take you to the sanatorium for medical attention."

"Oh, what silly nonsense," Frau Fischer replies crossly. "There is nothing wrong with *this* old bird!"

"It is very important."

"I don't care how important you think it is. I shan't go!" She stamps a tiny foot. "I am not going anywhere near that stinking place."

"The sanatorium does not stink," says the nurse, returning her implements to her bag.

"No, I'm certain it doesn't stink," I add. "And they'll just keep an eye on you until you're better. And then you can come back here – if you want to." I glance at Crunch and Grind. They're looking at me under heavy eyebrows. I carry on regardless. "And if you were in Edenburg," I say, unable to stop myself, "Raphael might be able to come and see you every day!" I shouldn't have said the last bit. How can I promise that? And Raphael might not even feel well enough to visit her. Or worse, the medical staff at the hospital might spot something wrong, and try to examine *him*!

I open my mouth to try to retract what I just said, but Frau Fischer jumps in.

"Oh, my boy!" she exclaims, clapping her hands together. "Well, if that's the case, what are we waiting for?" She throws her blankets to the floor and stands up too quickly. Immediately, she starts to topple. I rush to her side and grab an arm to stop her from pitching forward, and the nearest nurse grabs the other. We stand for a moment with Frau Fischer wobbling between us, her legs bowing at the knees.

"We will have to carry her," the nurse holding her other elbow shouts to her sister, who has already removed the stretcher from her back and is lying it on the floor in readiness, as if fully expecting this would be the outcome of their visit.

"Ja," she says, her head down, checking the straps are all open.

"Will he be able to visit me today?" Frau Fischer says, as we guide her towards the stretcher.

"I'm not sure, but I'll ask him," I say.

I tell myself the most important thing is that she gets medical attention. And Raphael might feel better soon, and might agree to see her. He does seem to quite like her.

Getting Frau Fischer down to the floor and on to the

stretcher takes many minutes of cajoling and a hundred promises that we won't let her fall. Eventually she is strapped on safely, glancing about nervously. Crunch and Grind take an end each, bend their knees in a well-rehearsed routine, and after a loud heave-ho, lift Frau Fischer into the air. She lets out a little shriek and grabs hold of the long wooden poles at the sides.

As we leave the cottage she cries out. "Oh, what about Olga?" She twists round to look for her goat. "Oh, my Olga! I can't leave my Olga behind!"

Of course we cannot leave the goat behind. How could I have forgotten? I look at Crunch and Grind, but they both shrug, as if the goat is not their problem. Frau Fischer starts to try to climb out of the stretcher, but the nurses have lashed her to the canvas too tightly. She wriggles in frustration. "I can't leave my Olga," she wails, turning to me.

"I know," I say. "We'll just have to take her with us."

"Can she come to the sanatorium?"

I glance at Crunch and Grind, who shake their heads. "Well, we can ask them," I say. "And if they don't say yes, we'll find somewhere else for her to go." I wonder if Raphael's father will take the goat in. They have a lean-to at the side of their house where they store their logs. I'm sure there would be space for a goat there.

"Well, if they won't let her in, then I shan't go in either."

"The goat will be looked after," Crunch or Grind says.

I unhook Olga from her tether and take her to Frau Fischer's side, like a dog. She's stronger than she looks and tugs at the rope.

"Ah, you're a good girl," Frau Fischer says to me with a gummy smile, scratching Olga behind her ears. "Hold tight, mind. She's a strong one. Not like Hettie; she was an angel on the lead. But, oh, she was the greediest goat in Bavaria!"

We begin a fast walk towards the forest. Crunch and Grind walk just as quickly as they did on the way out here.

"Will there be food in the sanatorium?" Frau Fischer says after a moment's silence.

"Ja," says Crunch or Grind.

"Will there be Jägerschnitzel?" she says. "Ooh, I love Jägerschnitzel!" She smacks her lips. "I haven't had it for years!" She turns back to me. "It used to be my speciality," she says, her eyes shining, "when I was a girl."

"There might be," I say, glancing at Crunch and Grind for confirmation.

They ignore me, their eyes flicking from side to side

and up towards the treetops.

"I've heard the food there is excellent," I lie.

Crunch or Grind pulls a face and rolls her eyes, but says nothing.

"And when will *he* be able to come and see me?"

When I don't reply, Frau Fischer twists round to look at me. Noticing how I'm struggling to keep hold of Olga, she laughs. "She's strong, that one. Not like Agnes. *She* was a lazy goat. Or was that…? I lose track. That's the problem with being old. Too many goats!" She shakes her head and mutters to herself as if trying to retrieve a memory from long ago. We plod along in silence as Frau Fischer drifts away to another, perhaps happier, time.

"They was crying, you know," she says suddenly, reaching out towards me, beckoning me to come closer.

"Who was crying?" I say, trotting to her side and leaning in to hear her.

"The angels," she hisses. "When they brought the boy. They didn't want to leave their baby like that in an owls' nest. But how could he live up there without wings? He'd fall to Earth like a stone!"

My heart begins to race. Is she talking about Raphael's parents? Were they forced to leave their angel baby in the forest because he was born without wings?

"What did they look like? The angels?" I whisper,

169

leaning in more closely, still clinging to Olga's lead.

"Like him," Frau Fischer says. "Eyes as bright and just as blue."

"But did they look like people?" I say quietly, my face now inches from hers.

"Yes, if people are filled with so much light you can see their innards, and have wings from head to toe."

I remember how Raphael briefly seemed to light up at his cottage, but I certainly couldn't see all his innards. I wonder if she might be exaggerating a little. Crunch and Grind are still charging ahead, tight-lipped and unspeaking, not even glancing at the frail old woman they're carrying. I know that Papa often doesn't hear me if he's absorbed in a task. Maybe Crunch and Grind are the same.

Olga pulls at her lead, and I wrap it more tightly round my hand, wincing as the rough rope cuts into my skin.

It's starting to snow again and as the sun morphs into an orb of deep red, scarlet tendrils dance about the fat snowflakes floating down through the trees. Olga tugs at the lead again and I swear at her under my breath, yanking her towards me. She bleats as if calling to someone far away.

"Oh, you shut your muzzle, you noisy creature," Frau Fischer says. "What are you bleating about this time?

Are you hungry?" She looks up at the nurse nearest her head. "Do they feed goats in the sanatorium, dear?"

Briefly distracted by the thought of a goat in a hospital, I catch my foot on something protruding from the ground, half buried in the snow. I pitch forward and land painfully on a gnarled lump of tree root. I let go of Olga's lead and, before I can grab it again, she trots off into the forest.

"Verdammt!" one of the nurses says.

"Dumme Ziege!" says the other.

"Oh, dear me, no!" Frau Fischer cries. "Olga, come back!"

I pick myself up and brush snow from my knees. "I'll get her," I say, trying not to feel too frightened at the thought of venturing off into the forest on my own, but pleased to have an excuse to get away for a moment to think. "If I'm quick, I should be able to catch up with her."

"Nein!" Crunch and Grind both shout, beginning to lower Frau Fischer to the ground.

"She's just an old goat," I say. "How fast can she be? I'll catch her up in no time." And without waiting for them to agree I race after Olga.

"Olga!" I call. "Wait!"

She bleats again, but sounds even further away now.

I scramble through undergrowth, shouting for the old goat, heading deeper and deeper into the forest, my mind whizzing with Frau Fischer's words. I know I shouldn't have followed the goat on my own. But what else could I do? Frau Fischer won't go anywhere without Olga. And she can't stay another night alone in the forest, suffering from whatever ailment Crunch and Grind thinks she has, with those birds hovering over her roof.

I stop and listen for the goat, my eyes searching the trees for movement. The firs are so dense here it is difficult to see more than a few yards ahead. I squint upwards, trying to gauge the position of the sun, certain I'm heading east. Hearing a distant bleat, I run towards the sound.

A dark shadow passes above me and a chill runs down my spine. I keep running, not daring to look up. What was I thinking? Crunch or Grind could have come after Olga. But it's too late to worry about that now.

The ground ahead begins to rise, and I find myself clambering up the long ridge on the eastern fringe of the forest, towards the old castle that looms fortress-like over the treetops. I spot Olga in the distance, and realise with horror that she is heading straight towards it.

"Olga," I hiss again, as loudly as I dare. "Come back now."

The last time I saw the castle a black bird flew out of one of its windows. Of course it was probably just a crow, but still I approach cautiously, keeping low to the ground.

The castle seems to grow from the rock on which it stands, making it difficult to tell where the rock stops and the castle starts. The squat tower at one end has two small windows on its upper levels, a pair of eyes surveying the forest, and a large central cavity below that gapes wide like a scream.

My blood runs cold. I have the most horrible sensation that I'm being watched. I glance back at the forest, wondering how far away Crunch and Grind and Frau Fischer are now. They're probably still plodding towards Edenburg. They won't be worrying about me.

I glance at the sun again. It's so low now it seems to be resting on the tops of the trees. I step hesitantly towards the castle, swearing under my breath. Why has Olga chosen here, of all the places to run?

Grim clouds gather above, casting the castle into deep shadow.

I turn back and survey the forest. My house in the distance, perched high on its rock, beckons to me to come home.

Olga scales the final and steepest slope of rock that

runs up to the castle door, bleating down at me as she reaches flat ground close to the main entrance, as if calling me to join in with her fun.

I scramble up the jagged rock face, scraping my knees as I haul myself up, clinging to climbing plants and mossy outcrops, praying they'll take my weight. Goats. I've never liked them. What was Olga thinking, climbing up here?

Eventually, breathless and bruised, I haul myself over the top of the rock.

A high caw shatters the silence. My heart misses a beat. I force myself to look up, but it is just a crow leaping about on the castle's broken battlements.

Olga trots confidently towards the castle, her spiky tail held high, flicking her back legs out joyfully as she leaps through the entrance.

Instinct tells me to run. To get away from this place as quickly as I can, back home to Papa, and Raphael, and Mother. But the stupid goat bleats again.

I step through the threshold into a large wide courtyard. The ground is uneven here, with fallen stones and bushes growing through what must have once been a floor. It appears to be utterly deserted.

A light wind whips up behind me and wraps round my body like a cool embrace.

I creep round the perimeter of the courtyard, my heart pounding, my ears straining for the tiniest sound. A fragile bleat comes from a corner of the courtyard near a narrow doorway into the tower.

I run towards it and take a deep breath before stepping into the building. "Olga," I hiss as loudly as I dare. I look about as my eyes adjust to the darkness. The earthy floor is soft and damp, and small deep footprints show me the route Olga has taken. I trip on a stone and stumble, and, as I reach out to save myself, my fingers make contact with cold, slippery castle walls. I wipe my hand on my dress and creep forward, cursing the goat.

I hear another bleat in the distance and take another hesitant step forward, turning back briefly to be sure I can still find my way out. A shaft of light shines through the doorway I came in. I should be able to find my way back if I get lost.

But Olga has completely disappeared. The floor becomes dry and stony and her hoof prints disappear. I tiptoe along the darkening corridor, my arms stretched out in front of me.

A shaft of light at the end of the corridor draws me deeper into the castle. I wonder if the light might be coming in through another entrance on the building's western elevation. I step towards it and eventually find myself in what must be the castle's tower. It is a vast room with high, rough-hewn stone walls that stretch all the way up to the battlements at the top. Lichen and mosses cling to the walls, creeping into deep, dark holes that must have once been home to the original floors of the tower.

A shadow passes above, sending a shiver down my spine. I glance up, but see nothing more than dark clouds gathering anxiously overhead, willing me to get out.

A sudden sharp bleat from shadows in the far corner makes me jump. It's Olga!

I run towards her. "Olga!" I whisper. She bleats again, more loudly than before. "Shhh," I hiss as loudly as I dare. "Stay there!" I just need to get close enough to grab her lead.

As I approach, I get the distinct impression that she wants me to rescue her, and wonder if she's as frightened as me. As soon as I'm close enough, I jump on to the long rope tether dangling from her collar, grab it and tug her towards me. She follows without objection.

We are halfway back across the room when something changes. It's just a peculiar feeling at first. But then the temperature drops. I gasp as a blast of icy air sweeps across my cheeks. The room sinks into darkness. I freeze, willing Olga not to utter a sound. She looks at me, her amber eyes wide with fear.

A sharp sound from above breaks the silence, cutting through the air like a whip. I force myself to look up.

The entire top of the tower is now a mass of birds. Giant birds. Not rooks or crows.

They are the Sturmfalken. And there are hundreds of them.

They are watching me through bright, unblinking eyes.

For a moment we remain like this, suspended in time. I move as slowly as I dare, hoping not to spook them. But then they dive towards me like a volley of arrows and I drop Olga's tether and run, racing out of the tower and down the corridor, desperately praying I'll remember how to get out of here. The sound of Olga's hooves on the stone floor reassures me she is close behind.

I seem to be gaining a lead on them. Their wings are so vast it is as if they are struggling to fly down the corridor.

I spot a shaft of light ahead. It is the entrance I came in through. I race towards it and burst out into the daylight.

I run across the courtyard and out of the main castle entrance. I quickly turn back and see that only a couple of birds are following me. Olga takes a leap down the sheer rock in front of us. I have no choice but to follow her.

I close my eyes and jump, and tumble helplessly, crying in pain as I bounce down the side of the ridge, desperately trying to grab hold of anything to break my fall.

A sharp outcrop at the base of the ridge races towards me. Screaming, I twist and turn, trying to control my descent, but I only seem to fall faster. I hit the rock and the world falls silent.

★

I am rocking from side to side. Strong arms grip me hard, holding me so tightly I cannot shake free. My head knocks against something solid. I realise I am slung over someone's shoulder. With each step they take my forehead crashes painfully against their back. Every part of me hurts. A harsh bleat nearby startles me. I force my eyes open. The world is upside down and my only view is of the forest floor, woollen socks and sturdy brown-leather boots stomping through the snow. I wriggle to try to free myself and the person carrying me mutters something under their breath.

"Ah, there you are!" says a voice full of brightness. "I said she'd be all right, didn't I?"

The strong arms lower me to the ground. I try to stand

up but my legs buckle underneath me, and I collapse with a thud into the deep snow.

I look up, a little surprised to be met by the bright eyes of Frau Fischer and the heavy eyebrows and downturned mouths of Crunch and Grind.

"And you brought Olga back to me," she says, sitting on her stretcher in the snow. "You're a good girl, you are. I knew you'd bring Olga back."

Crunch or Grind makes a harrumphing noise. "She should have listened to us. It is not safe out here."

"But I couldn't let it run away, and you were carrying Frau Fischer," I mutter.

"We would have waited. You shouldn't have run."

I look up at the sky, but the clouds that were hanging over the castle seem to have dispersed altogether. "Did you see all those birds?" I say. I can't imagine they could have simply disappeared. They *must* have followed me as I tumbled down the ridge.

They shake their heads grimly. "Just you and the goat," one says.

I look at them, standing over me with their arms crossed, and wonder briefly if I might have imagined the whole thing. But I can still smell the birds. I know I didn't imagine it.

But why didn't they follow me? I can't believe they'd

willingly let me escape.

Olga is now lashed to Crunch or Grind's wide leather belt. The nurse flicks the tether, and the goat steps obediently towards her. I glare at it.

"We need to get back to town before it gets dark," she says to me. "Can you walk?"

I nod, not daring to speak in case I cry.

"Right, you two, heave-ho," says Frau Fischer, lying back as Crunch and Grind lift her from the ground, a pair of giant oak trees with a threadbare hammock strung between them. I follow them, as they march ahead with Olga trotting at their side.

Chapter Twenty-Three

After taking Frau Fischer to the sanatorium, I limp home to find Raphael looking as miserable as when I left him, looking out over the forest with the cherub at the window. He turns when he sees me and she flies into my arms.

"Cassie, what happened to you?"

I haven't had a chance to look at myself yet, but my temple is throbbing from where it must have hit the rocky outcrop.

"I had a tumble. It's nothing."

"It isn't nothing," he says.

He examines my face and I find myself blushing. He reaches out and gently touches my forehead. The warmth from his fingers is like a hot compress, and strangely my pain seems to ease.

"It doesn't look too bad," he says. "It's just a bit swollen."

I nod. "It's feeling better already."

"And how is Frau Fischer?"

I tell him how we carried her from the forest, and most of what she said about him. As I recount everything that happened at the castle, and the hundreds of birds in the tower, I start to worry I shouldn't have told him about the gathering Sturmfalken. He looks so unhappy and frightened, I don't think I can bear to tell him about his mother weeping as she left him as a baby in the forest too. And maybe Frau Fischer was wrong about that part. She does seem quite muddled.

He sinks into the desk chair. "I hate to ask you this, but would you mind taking my bindings off, just for a little while? I feel so constrained like this."

"Of course!" I say, steeling myself for the sight of his wounds once again.

I untuck the end of the binding, and as gently as I can, slowly unwrap it. Raphael is generating so much heat I worry he might be developing a fever. I place my hand on his forehead but it is cool to my touch. The heat is coming from his wounds. The binding is sticky with yellow fluid. It doesn't smell unpleasant but makes unwrapping the sheet difficult. He gasps each time I tug at it.

I detach the last piece and let it fall to the floor.

"Thank you," he says. "If I could reach it, I would do it myself."

"I know you would do the same for me," I say. "It's nothing."

I wipe up a trickle of fluid running down his back, and as I do so a large feather springs out from one of the wounds, making me jump. It is as if the thing is alive! Another feather emerges.

"What can you see?" he cries. "I can feel something moving."

I don't reply.

"Please tell me," he says. "I need to know."

"They *have* grown a little more," I say. "But they're still just feathers. Not wings. But the new feathers do seem to be getting bigger."

I don't dare touch the wounds. They are starting

to heal round the edges, almost as if they have been hemmed by a skilled seamstress. And the bleeding has stopped. But fresh blood is still visible deep within the cavities.

"We need to work out how to stop this," I say. "There must be a way." I suddenly have an idea. "Would you like me to pluck a feather out? If I can, we could remove the others too. And then we could call Crunch and Grind, and they could stitch you up. And then we could go back to the way we were." I glance up at the cherub. "Well, not quite the way we were."

"You could try," he says, sounding unconvinced.

"Promise you'll tell me if it hurts."

"Oh, I will."

The feathers are wet and slippery, so I dry them with a clean-looking corner of the old binding. The metallic smell has gone, replaced now by the scent of crushed almonds. But despite this, I still have to fight back the feeling of nausea welling up inside me.

I choose a suitable-looking feather and wrap the sheet round my hand like a glove.

I tug at the feather sharply.

Raphael screams – a horrible ear-splitting howl that makes my stomach lurch.

"I'm so sorry!" I cry, jumping back and dropping the

binding to the floor.

He falls silent, his face a deathly shade of green-grey.

"I don't think we should try that again," he says eventually.

"Of course. It was a silly idea," I say. "I could saw them off with a knife. Do you think that would hurt so much?"

He sinks his head into his hands and weeps. "But they'll keep coming, Cassie. I know they will. Like sails unfurling on a ship. They are inevitable."

His use of the word *unfurling* triggers a memory. Of something not quite right. Something in the wrong place. I rack my brains. And then I remember. "I just need to get something from Papa's workshop," I say. "I won't be a moment."

I race across the owlery and fling the workshop door open. The monkey is still there, the deathly stare still etched across its face. I toss it on to the workbench, and find the pamphlet in the same place. I grab it and read the cover.

The Final Unfurling.

I breathlessly flick through its pages, wondering where it could have come from. It can't be anything to do with Papa; there's nothing in here about taxidermy. I run back to the library and drop it on the desk in front of Raphael. He picks it up hesitantly, and I lean over his shoulder as we look through it together.

"It's when you said the word *unfurling*," I say. "It reminded me of this."

Handwritten notes and diagrams fill each page. There is a date on the inside cover. 1824. The year Ramiel died.

Raphael glances at me. "This is what's happening to me, Cassie. About my wings growing!" He looks confused. "But why would it be here? In your house?"

"I've no idea," I say. "Or how long it's been in Papa's workshop."

We sit in silence as we flick through the pamphlet. Each page is filled with scribbled, frantic notes – a stream of consciousness more than anything coherent. The handwriting is so poor it is difficult to make sense of it in parts. Some pages are no more than a blur of black ink.

I pick out the words that are still legible.

Great pain and distress... Angels... Years... Months... Days...

We turn over the pages together and find a section with a series of hand-drawn diagrams. The author has sketched the various stages in the unfurling of an angel's wings. It seems that Raphael is at the first stage – what they describe as *the breaking through* and that there are many more stages after this. There are also recommendations on how to care for new wings and keep them free from infection. There is even a recipe for a poultice to ensure their even growth, as an angel's wings must be perfectly symmetrical to ensure safe flight.

There are lists of *Do Nots* throughout, with little stars scribbled around them to emphasise their importance. The first one, underlined many times, is: *Do not attempt to pluck a feather from the body. This will damage the feather's shaft and inflict unnecessary suffering on the angel.* I feel a stab of remorse.

There are diagrams showing the internal anatomy of an angel and notes informing the reader that they are quite different to normal people, despite their outward similarity. I wonder how the author was able to conduct such a detailed study of the internal mechanics of an angel.

The bones are strong and sturdy, but populated with small bubbles of air, thus allowing the angel to rise when necessary.

The heart is larger than a human heart, allowing an angel to feel immense compassion and love for those around them. This also gives them considerable physical endurance.

The brain of an angel has a large frontal lobe, meaning they are capable of great empathy and kindness.

An angel may have an imposing physical presence.

The author is describing Raphael – or someone like him. *He* has an immense physical presence. And he is kind. Kinder than anyone I know.

I turn the page and my heart sinks. The page is entitled *Impediments to the Rise of an Angel*. An encircled sketch of many Sturmfalken dominates the page, with more stars drawn around it for emphasis. Underneath are the words: *The Sturmfalken are the greatest threat to a rising angel. They will do everything in their power to prevent its accession.*

Accession. Rise.

Both words mean the same thing.

"I just don't understand it," Raphael says. "Why would the Sturmfalken be interested in what happens to an angel?"

I shake my head. None of this makes any sense.

"There is something else," I say hesitantly. "Something Frau Fischer said."

I have to tell him. He needs to know.

He looks at me anxiously.

"She was talking again about the angels that came down the night she found you. It was a woman and a man, Raphael." I pause before continuing. "She said they wept as they left you."

His eyes are wide. "Do you think they might have

been my parents?" he whispers, his hands beginning to tremble.

"It's possible," I say, trying to remember exactly what else Frau Fischer said. "She said an angel baby without wings would fall to Earth like a stone. Maybe that's why they brought you here, Raphael. Maybe you couldn't survive wherever they live without wings."

"So my wings decided to come in their own time. Perhaps they were always there, Cassie, hidden away, waiting for their big moment."

I smile, wishing I knew what to say to make him feel better.

The cherub flutters her wings, rises from the desk and lands with a gentle thud on Raphael's knee. He wraps his arms round her and rests his cheek on the top of her head. I want to take her from him, to hold her myself, to feel the comfort she gives, but he needs her more than I do.

"We need to stop this," I say decisively, flicking through the final pages of the pamphlet. "There must be something in here on how to stop the process. It's your body, Raphael. You must have a say in this! If we cannot remove your wings, maybe we can bind them so tightly they cannot grow. We cannot just accept this."

He looks away and shakes his head, but says nothing.

I look at the cherub. Her eyes look heavy, as if she is about to nod off in Raphael's arms. "You have to help us. Can't you see he doesn't wish to be an angel?"

She looks away from me too.

"I don't think we can stop it, Cassie," Raphael says quietly.

"But if we can just stop your wings growing—"

"But it is more than my wings. It is all of me. If you cut my wings, or stunt their growth, they will come again. We cannot stop it."

"But could we not hide them then?" I'm beginning to sound desperate, but I don't care. "Let them grow, but conceal them? I wouldn't tell a soul."

He shakes his head. "But I am what I am, Cassie, even if I hide my wings. And I think that's why the cherub's here. To help me."

"But why did she come to *me*? Why didn't she go to *your* house in the thunderstorm?"

"I don't know, Cassie!" he cries. "I don't know anything any more."

I glance at his back and peer into an open wound. "Is it still sore?"

He nods miserably.

I suddenly remember the bowl of gloop in Grandma's room. "Crunch and Grind left some sort of poultice for Grandma," I say. "A balm for her bedsores. Do you think that might help?"

Raphael shrugs. "I guess we could give it a try. It couldn't make it any worse."

I slip into Grandma's room and find the bowl where Crunch or Grind left it. A crust has formed on the top, but otherwise it looks just the same.

Back in the library, I scoop up a dollop of the balm, take a deep breath and ease it into Raphael's wing cavities with my fingers, terrified all the while I might be doing something to make him worse. He gasps.

"Have I hurt you?" I say, my heart in my mouth.

"No, it's wonderful, Cassie," he says, his whole body seeming to sigh.

I dip my fingers into the gloop and slather more over his whole back, coating the feathers and the edges of the wounds too. As Raphael's shoulders relax I feel mine do too.

"I wonder what's in it," I say, holding my fingers to my nose, breathing it in. It smells a little minty, and of the earth, almost like the forest after heavy rain. "And how lucky Crunch and Grind left so much of it for Grandma," I say, realising I'm grinning.

Chapter Twenty-Four

In the morning I go to see Grandma. She's neatly tucked under her sheet and an eiderdown. Small shallow breaths and the rhythmic groan of the bellows are the only signs she is still alive. I lean over and kiss her forehead.

She opens her eyes. "Hello, darling. Is that you?" she says, looking a little disorientated.

"Yes, it's me," I say, perching on the edge of the chair next to the bed. "How are you feeling today?" It's a silly question with her like this.

"The same, thank you, darling."

Her false teeth sit abandoned in a glass on the bedside table. She bought them from a strange-smelling shop in a back street in München years ago. Papa said afterwards they'd been taken from the mouths of fallen French soldiers at the Battle of Waterloo. Appalled and astonished, we always referred to them after that as her "Waterloo Teeth". I used to scream with laughter when she gnashed them at me, revelling in the horror of their gruesome past. How I'd love to see those teeth back in action one last time.

We sit in silence for a while, listening to the creak and stretch of the pump's bellows, while I decide what to say.

It's suddenly stifling in here, and I shove my chair back and walk to the window to let in some fresh air.

"Grandma?" I say.

"Yes, darling?"

"I think there might be something strange going on. In the forest. And in the house." I want to tell her everything that's happened, but I don't want to frighten her. She may know nothing about any of this.

She looks away from me and sighs. "What sort of strange thing?"

Her voice is so weak I have to strain my ears to hear her.

"Well, I'm not sure, but there are some odd things happening with the owls. And I've found some books in the library that are a little confusing."

She taps the bed next to her.

I push the window closed and sit next to her.

"Has a cherub come?" she asks quietly.

"Y-you know about the cherub?" I stammer.

"I know what its arrival heralds," she says, her eyes welling with tears. Her hands have begun to shake. "It's happened before, you see."

"It's happened before!? And when was that?"

"Not long before I was born," she says. "It came for Ramiel. It was his time, and he had to go. The poor boy didn't have a choice."

"But you said Ramiel died, Grandma!"

"Yes, he did die. It was his time to rise, you see, but it was interrupted." She shakes her head sadly. "Everyone was terribly distressed, as you would expect."

"And what do you mean by 'time to rise'?" I ask quietly. I thought the cherub had come to help Raphael turn into an angel, but has she come to take him away?

"It's when an angel is called home to their real parents. Oh, I hoped the day would never come." She's weeping

Fledgling

quietly now, tears tumbling down her cheeks. I pick up her handkerchief and wipe them away. But I don't understand why she's crying. Ramiel died before she was born and she doesn't know Raphael very well.

"And do you know where they rise to, Grandma?"

"Oh, I don't know, darling. It's a long, long way away. Up in the firmament somewhere. Their celestial kingdom. But they never want to go. And who can blame them?" She sighs. "But you mustn't worry about silly old me. I'm worried about you, darling. You're going to have to be brave when it happens."

I nod. "So have there been many of these angels over the years?"

"Just Ramiel that I know of. And now the next one. But there'll always be more." She closes her eyes. "Once their wings have grown, their family want them back. Oh, the poor wingless angels."

"And what interrupted Ramiel's rising?" I say hesitantly. "How did he die?"

"They came for him to stop him rising."

"*They?*"

"Those awful birds. Driven only by jealousy and a desire for more celestial space. I only know what my parents told me, of course, and they told me very little. They, like poor old Walter Engel, hoped there would never be another one."

"Celestial space?' I whisper, struggling to keep up. "Is that the same as the firmament?"

"Yes, darling, something like that. You know how men fight over territory on Earth? That dreadful war that broke your poor papa? It's much the same, except that the angels are not very good at fighting, and there really aren't enough of them. That's why it's so important they go home when they're ready. Why they rise. Why we mustn't stop them."

"Well, I'm going to try," I say. They can't take Raphael from his home. From everything and everyone he knows. And he's not a fighter. I've never known anyone more gentle.

She doesn't reply immediately, but eventually she says, "It is like trying to stop day turning into night. I have learned to accept it will happen again, and you must too."

I say nothing, but I will find a way to stop it. There must be a way.

"Why didn't you tell me all this sooner, Grandma?" I say, trying not to feel cross with her. How could she know all this and not think to tell me, or Mother or Papa?

"I'm sorry, darling, I didn't want to frighten you... And I hoped it might never happen again."

"But does everyone else know?"

She looks away and shakes her head, her eyes glistening with tears. The effort of talking seems to have worn her out. I sit for a while watching her chest fluttering, and breathe in and out deeply to control the panic rising within me. When I am absolutely certain she is asleep I lean over and kiss her forehead.

She mumbles something in my ear.

"What's that, Grandma?"

"Don't forget," she says.

"Don't forget?"

"Don't forget to sing…"

"But I don't sing. I can't sing."

"Oh yes you do. And you can. Never forget that, Cassie," she whispers. "It's the only way you'll beat them."

"Beat who, Grandma?"

"Sing – sing – sing," she mutters under her breath, as if addressing someone far away.

I leave her, now even more terrified about what Raphael is going to face.

Chapter Twenty-Five

As I walk back through the owlery, Grandma's words still echoing through my mind, I suddenly freeze. Someone, or something, is watching me.

Maybe it's just Papa in the workshop. I open the door and peek inside. The macaque monkey is still where I left it, lying on the workbench, staring up at the ceiling. A badger lies spread-eagled nearby – a work in progress with lumps in all the wrong places. Otherwise the room is empty. I close the door quietly and tiptoe back through the owlery, short hairs pricking at the back of my neck, not daring to look round.

I find Raphael in the library, looking out of the window. New feathers have sprouted from his back.

"She knows," I say.

"Your grandma? About me?" He looks shocked. "What did she say?"

I tell him what Grandma said, but not about what happened to Ramiel. I pick the book up from the desk. "And that explains why *this* is here, and all the other books about angels."

"So the same thing happened to your great-great-uncle! But why is this not common knowledge?"

"I don't know," I say. "Would any family wish to tell people they had an angel in their midst? Maybe they'd be worried his discovery would cause unwanted attention."

"Perhaps. So he was Walter Engel's son?"

"Yes, he was, but…" I remember what Grandma said about Ramiel. "I think he might have been adopted, Raphael. Like you."

"Really? Perhaps he was found in the forest too." He smiles. "So I'm not the only one, Cassie!"

We sit in silence for a while. The painting of Ramiel

is still tucked in my pocket. "There's something else," I say, pulling the portrait out and handing it to Raphael. "This is Ramiel."

Raphael takes it from me and squints at it. "But he looks exactly like me!" He examines the portrait of the boy more carefully, holding it up to the lamp. "How can that be?"

"I don't know," I say. "Perhaps you're related."

"Maybe we are," he says quietly. "Just separated by time."

He puts a hand over his mouth and looks at me intently for a few seconds before turning away.

"Did you find anything useful in here?" I say, turning the pages of the book.

"Just more gruesome details about the process of wing development."

"Anything about how to stop them growing?"

He shakes his head.

"I think there's something strange going on in the owlery," I say.

"What sort of thing?"

"I don't know. An unusual energy. Just now I felt as if I was being watched. It was horrible."

"Shall I come and look?"

"No, no, you need to rest." I don't add that I have no

wish to go back in there. "And I need to find something else first. I saw a book the other day. It didn't make any sense at the time. About owls. And taxidermy too, I think. Something about how stuffed owls can be used to predict future events."

What if the owls are trying to tell me something?

★

I find the book easily – *Damman's Rules for Taxidermy: The Arte of Preserving the Owle for the Divination of Celestial Energie*. The pages are worn, and some are glued together with a dried-out, crispy substance, giving it the feel of an old family recipe book. Detailed diagrams demonstrating techniques for the preservation of owls fill its pages. I read a chapter called *Preserving the Owle for the Divination of an Ominous Event*. The final chapter is entitled *An Event to Precipitate the Awakening of the Owles*.

There are neatly written notes in the margins, with suggested quantities of preservation chemicals. This is my great-great-grandfather's handwriting. I'd recognise it anywhere; it's on every label in the owlery.

I pass the book to Raphael. A distant crash of thunder shakes the house and a deep gloom settles across the library. As Raphael is thrown into darkness, for just a fleeting moment he seems to glow. After a second the illusion disappears.

"*An Event to Precipitate the Awakening of the Owles,*" he reads, before closing the book and placing it carefully on the desk. "It seems that someone might have set up some sort of early-warning system."

"But what are they warning us about?"

"Maybe it's about what's happening to me."

"Because of your wings growing?"

"Possibly," he says. "But why would we need to be warned? Isn't it obvious? And why here? In your house?"

I shrug, wondering if Mother knows more about the owls than she's been letting on. "Would you like me to bind you again? In case someone comes in?"

"We probably should," he says, looking reluctant to be trussed up again.

I apply more balm to his wounds and wrap a long clean strip of sheet round him.

"How does it feel now?"

"The balm is helping," he says. "Thank you." He looks at me through eyes that gleam like sapphires.

A low hum starts up in the owlery. "What's that?" I whisper.

"I don't know," he says, suddenly wide-eyed with fear.

As quietly as I can, I pull the door open just an inch

and peer into the owlery.

It is the owls.

They are singing.

Chapter Twenty-Six

The house is silent as we walk into the owlery, as if it's holding its breath – listening, like us, to the owls and their song. The cherub lands with a thud on my shoulder. Her breath is light and guarded, as if she is listening too. My breathing begins to settle, but my heart still beats like a drum.

A crash of thunder makes me jump. The storm is getting closer.

I open my mouth to say something, anything, to Raphael, but as our eyes meet he shakes his head, just slightly, as if to tell me to remain silent. He nods in the direction of Eric, the old eagle owl in the centre of the room. Something has changed about him, but it is difficult to tell in this light. I creep towards the owl, gripping the cherub like a shield. She is growling like a wild cat.

The hum of the owls is slow and quiet and mournful, like a chant at a requiem Mass. Is there a coded message in their tune? I can't remember anything about this in the book.

We reach the eagle owl and stand before him.

"He's changed," I whisper, peering through the glass of his display cabinet. "But I can't work out what it is."

Raphael examines him carefully. "I don't think I've looked at him that closely before. I couldn't say."

The owls fall silent.

A fog descends over my mind, making it impossible to make sense of what is happening around me. The air in the room is hot and heavy and invisible tendrils wrap round me, suffocating me. The room spins. I grip the cherub tightly and shiver. And then the strange feeling slips away.

"What was that?" I hiss.

"I don't think that was anything to do with her," Raphael whispers.

Whatever happened just now felt malevolent. I look at the eagle owl warily, certain this must be something to do with him.

"Look at his eyes, Raphael."

The cherub is growling again.

Raphael squints at the owl. "What about them?"

I push the cherub into his arms and run to the workshop. Pulling open the drawer labelled *Eagle owl eyes*, I pluck one out with shaking hands and rush back into the owlery. "Look," I say. "His eyes should be orange!" I hold the glass eye up between my thumb and forefinger. "Like this. An eagle owl's eyes are always orange!" I point at the stuffed eagle owl. "But *his* eyes are green. Something has happened to him, Raphael!"

We stare at the owl and he stares back at us.

And then he blinks.

I scream and the cherub screams too, as if imitating me.

My feet seem to be glued to the floor. I cannot move.

The room fills with colour, everything around me a maelstrom of light and sound. I try to force my lips closed to stop my screams, but I can't stop. Through my fractured vision, I can just make out Raphael staring at me with a look of horror. For every note I make the cherub duplicates it. I put my hands over my ears to try to block it all out.

The owls begin their funereal refrain again. Their hum is quiet and restrained alongside the screams the cherub and I are making. Raphael is the only one who is silent.

My voice rises steadily in pitch, as if I'm singing an arpeggio. What am I doing? Why can't I stop myself?

Raphael holds his hands over his ears. I try to say sorry to him, that I cannot help this, but I cannot form the words.

"Please stop," he pleads. "I can't bear it."

A flash of light briefly blinds me. And then there is an explosion.

The sound of shattering glass fills the room.

Tiny shards of glass flutter above us like butterflies, and as they pass through the narrow beam of lamplight from the library, they seem to burst into flames.

Only then does my screaming stop.

Time slows. My movements become cumbersome and heavy. The fragments of glass that have been swirling above my head float down like confetti and settle in sparkling pools on the floor.

I fall to my knees, the cherub wrapped tightly in my arms. Glass cuts into my skin. I push my hair back from my face and look up at the eagle owl above me.

He is alive.

His glass case is in smithereens, and he stands stiffly on his perch, looking down at us.

He spreads his vast wings wide, as if stretching after a long sleep, revealing a seam down the front of his body. It begins to pull apart, exposing ancient stitches. Through this narrow gap emerges something dark and shiny. The seam widens further, allowing night-black feathers to flick out. Then glinting gun-metal grey talons force their way through the owl's belly and tear impatiently at what remains of the owl.

Finally the eagle owl explodes and a great feathered beast many times its size appears from within it. The discarded husk of the owl falls to the bottom of the display case and lands on glass-encrusted mossy stones, and dusty fading ferns.

A giant hawklike bird stands in its place and stretches its wings. It looks about the room, sniffing.

It is a Sturmfalke. I know it. But it is vast compared to the bird that attacked me in the forest. Its beak is long and sharp and strong-looking, like that of a vulture. It could tear me to pieces in seconds. The smell of rancid flesh fills the room.

The creature's head rotates suddenly as its gaze darts about the room. Its eyes are wide but appear unfocused. I barely dare to breathe. It stretches out its wings, revealing a giant wingspan. Its claws grip tightly to its perch.

I remain frozen in front of it, aware of Raphael quietly moving behind one of the other display cases, beckoning to me to follow him.

It seems not to see us and sniffs.

The cherub frees herself from my grip and hovers in front of the bird, her beating wings sending tiny slithers of glass scuttling along the floor. The rancid smell appears to be receding. Within seconds the sweet scent of almonds fills the room, reminding me briefly of Emaline's sticky frangipane tarts. It wraps round me like a cloak.

A lost memory of the forest attack returns. I am screaming. Screaming so loudly it takes my breath away. I can almost hear it now – long and high and loud, like the sound that Mother sometimes makes in her music room.

The Sturmfalke beats its wings, as if testing them for strength, before slowly rising from its perch. Its wings move in a rhythmic motion, scattering glass and making my hair flutter. It hovers above me, its black-tipped razor-like talons and leathery yellow feet just inches from my face. I hold my breath.

It shrieks, a slow, mournful noise that reveals a pink and blue tongue, which flicks in and out like a lizard. It stretches its wide muscular legs, as if relieving cramp after a long sleep. It lands on the floor next to me and looks about, still seemingly oblivious to us. I barely dare to breathe. It beats its wide tail against the floor, causing the display cases in the room to rattle and the house to shake.

Then it rises up above us and flies towards the window. It squeezes itself on to the windowsill and pecks at the window with its beak until it gives way and topples with a crash to the rock below.

The creature glances briefly back across the room, before leaping out of the window and disappearing from view.

We sit in silence for some time, staring speechlessly at the shattered window.

"What just happened?" I say, getting up shakily. I peer out of the gaping hole in the wall, then lean against the wall to steady myself.

Raphael is ashen. "It seems there was a Sturmfalke

hiding inside that owl."

"But how is that possible?"

He shakes his head. "I don't know, Cassie."

"And what was I doing?" I cry. "With the screaming? I couldn't stop myself." I angrily wipe the tears streaming down my face with my sleeve and sink to the floor. I bury my head in my hands.

When I look up again, the cherub is sitting cross-legged on the floor, eyes closed, as if the strangest thing in the world never happened.

I look at her carefully. "She did something," I whisper. "Just now. Something to protect us."

"Like the thing she did at my house?"

The scent of almonds still hangs in the air, and a thought occurs to me. "Raphael, that creature didn't seem able to see us. It was sniffing. Perhaps these things hunt by smell. Maybe they *entirely* rely on their sense of smell to hunt."

"So you think they can't see very well?"

I nod. "Maybe she stopped it being able to pick up our scent?"

"But it could find its way to the window."

"Maybe it was drawn to the light, like a moth."

Dark clouds jostle for space outside, throwing the room into darkness. Thunder rolls close by and a flash of lightning briefly lights up the room.

Did the cherub just save us? Or has the creature something else planned for us?

Chapter Twenty-Seven

The door swings open. It is Emaline, carrying a broom and a dustpan and brush. She walks in and closes the door quietly behind her.

I look at her, astonished. "Do you know what just happened, Emaline?"

She raises her brows and sets about sweeping the floor. She clears up the glass slowly and methodically, bending stiffly to scoop it up, revealing cosy-looking woollen stockings beneath her dress.

"Let me do that," I say.

She ignores me.

Once the floor is clear of glass, she peers out of the open window cavity. "So it went out of the window," she says.

I nod.

"Shame it didn't open it first."

"Emaline!" I say. "Do you know what it was? Did you see it?"

Raphael picks up what remains of the old eagle owl. Emaline takes it from him and turns it over, examining it closely.

"Emaline, we don't know what's going on," I say.

She tosses the eagle owl aside and begins to tidy up the base of the broken display case.

"Emaline," I say again, hobbling towards her. "Do you know what's happening?"

"I could hardly ignore that racket you were making," she says, her eyes slipping towards the door.

"I know that," I say, "but how did you know to bring a broom? And how do you know that something flew out of the window? We might have simply broken it ourselves!"

I stare at her, hands on hips, challenging her to answer.

"If you know what's happening, we need your help, because we really don't understand what's going on." I wave my hand around the room. "How could a creature climb inside a dead owl without anyone noticing?"

"Maybe he didn't climb inside," she says. "Maybe someone put him in there." She glares at me as if I'm somehow responsible. And with that she stomps out of the room, slamming the door behind her.

"Well, that was strange," Raphael says.

"She's often strange," I say.

I examine the remains of the broken display case.

"What's that?" Raphael says, leaning over my shoulder.

"What's what?"

"Look! There's a piece of card there – under that stone."

"It's probably an old label. It might have fallen off the owl years ago," I say, picking up the small yellowing label.

I turn it over. But it isn't a label. It's a tiny envelope, with two words written on the front, and an ancient-looking wax seal holding it closed.

It says, *Open immediately!*

Chapter Twenty-Eight

It is my great-great-grandfather's writing. I slide my finger under the seal and pop the envelope open. With trembling hands I extract a tiny handwritten note. I read it out loud.

"If you are reading this, you are in grave danger."

I glance at Raphael and take a deep breath before continuing.

"I implore you to absorb what I am about to tell you.

Concealed underneath this case is a voice-duplication machine."

Is this another of my great-great-grandfather's inventions? I often find mysterious contraptions lurking in cupboards or tucked away in dark corners, but this is something I have never heard of before. Frowning, I turn the card over.

"My eyesight is not what it once was. I am therefore leaving you a 'voice message' to explain a little more about your predicament."

Papa once dragged me to an exhibition of engines and machinery in München to look for a replacement part for the zip. It wasn't at all what we were expecting, and instead of discovering exciting inventions and spare parts, we found ourselves in great noisy halls filled with heavy industrial machinery. We felt quite out of place among the leagues of men with waxed moustaches, top hats and bulging order books. But strangely, in the midst of all this, we fell upon a stall demonstrating the latest musical paraphernalia from America. I distinctly remember a small crowd gathering round some sort of voice-recording device. Might my great-great-grandfather have created something similar?

"When you reveal the device," I read, *"turn the handle twenty times to hear my message. It will explain the perils*

you are about to face. That is all, and may God protect you."

It is signed Walter Engel.

"*God protect us?*" I whisper.

Raphael's face is inscrutable. "I think we need more than God on our side," he mutters.

I examine the display case, searching for a latch, but there is no obvious hinge or lock. I tap it with my knuckles. It's hollow. "How do I get into it?" I say. I kick the case in frustration and it shifts a little, revealing a thin line of dust along the floor. "That's it," I say. "It's just been placed over the device."

We rock the heavy display case backwards and forwards until we are able to slip our fingers underneath it. Taking a side each, we lift it away, revealing a large object shrouded in an old linen sheet. I rip the dusty fabric away, desperate to reveal what my great-great-grandfather hid in the owlery so long ago.

It is the strangest-looking contraption. At the base is a deep mahogany box about a foot or so long, with a vast brass trumpet-shaped cone protruding from it. A small green cylinder is bolted to the top of the box and this is attached to the narrow end of the trumpet with a series of rivets. I touch the cylinder hesitantly. It is slightly sticky – like soft wax. The cone gleams, despite all these years hidden in the dark. It smells of beeswax and metal and stale tobacco. The last person to touch this was probably my great-great-grandfather. It is similar to the machines at the exhibition, but looks home-made.

"I've seen something like this before," I whisper, remembering what the American had called his contraption. "It's a gramophone player."

Raphael looks at me. "A gramophone player?"

"Yes, a talking machine," I say. "For recording and replaying speech." I run my fingers along the brass handle on the side of the box.

I take hold of the handle and turn it twenty times as instructed, then release it. The waxy cylinder begins to rotate and a crackly voice emerges from the wide end of the trumpet. It is a man's voice. The voice of my great-great-grandfather. He's slowly counting from ten down to zero.

"It's as if he's within the machine," Raphael whispers, his eyes wide. He looks into the trumpet, perhaps expecting to find someone crouching inside it.

"A voice from another age," I say.

The recording is crackly, but I can hear him quite clearly. When he reaches zero, he clears his throat and begins.

"*This is Herr Walter Engel, recording this message to you in the owlery at Engel Rock on 14 January 1866.*

"*My dears, you are in grave danger. The creature I imprisoned within the eagle owl must have escaped, revealing my note hidden beneath his perch. His release will unleash a chain of events that will present a grave challenge to you, so listen carefully.*

"*It is many years since our son, Ramiel, was taken from us. There will be others like him, and my greatest wish is that you are better prepared than we were. I have adapted the house to help you or another like Ramiel.*"

I glance at Raphael. He is staring intently at the machine.

"*We adopted Ramiel after he was found in the forest as an infant, and he became brother to our natural-born son. Edenburg was alive at the time with stories about a pair of angels descending the night he was found, but we pooh-poohed this as nonsense. But the stories were true! Ramiel had been delivered to Earth as a wingless angel, to be raised among people – to learn the human traits of kindness, compassion and empathy, and to remain on Earth until his wings were sufficiently developed to join the host.*"

I glance at Raphael. He's blinking heavily.

"*The Sturmfalke imprisoned within the eagle owl is Strix, the most lethal and largest of that flock of foul celestial beasts. It is likely that dark forces are gathering around you as your angel prepares to rise. But Strix will be weak after his captivity, and it will take him a while to regain his strength. This will give you a little time to prepare.*

"I'm afraid he is a formidable opponent. To overpower and trap him, I doped him with a cocktail of taxidermy powders, followed by a solution of borax and formaldehyde to desiccate and paralyse him. But I am sorry to say I was unable to find a solution to destroy him completely. My great wish is that so long as he remains in this state, he will present no threat to my descendants."

"So how has he come back to life?" I say to Raphael as my great-great-grandfather pauses briefly, perhaps allowing us time to absorb his words.

"Maybe he somehow managed to rehydrate himself," he says.

"But I keep such a close eye on the owls. I'm sure I would have noticed if one was changing."

Raphael puts a finger to his lips as Walter Engel continues.

"The cherub sent to escort Ramiel to the kingdom failed in her mission, and he was killed by the Sturmfalken before he was able to rise. I will never forgive Strix for this."

His voice breaks as if he is fighting back tears. He blows his nose loudly.

"Did you know this?" Raphael says quietly.

I nod. "Grandma told me," I say. "But how could I

tell you, Raphael? And just because it happened once doesn't mean it will happen again!"

The recording continues.

"*I preserved the other owls in such a way that they would be activated in the presence of celestial energy, and that their orientation would change to 'face' a potential threat. This is an early-warning system.*"

I think of how many times the owls had changed position – how they had faced the forest. Was that because Raphael was there? Or because the *Sturmfalken* were gathering?

"*However much you wish things were different, you must allow your angel to follow their destiny, and protect them from those who wish to prevent them doing so.*

"*You will find a handle concealed under the floorboards immediately below this machine. If Strix has left the house, pull sharply on this with all your strength, and go immediately to the engine room. Once there, you will find further instructions.*

"*I am recording this with a heavy heart and wish that I might still be here to help you. You are about to face a great challenge. But you are not alone. Accept the help of the Guardians, if offered. They will be your closest allies. I do not wish to take up any more of your time as you have pressing needs to deal with. I wish you well. And God speed.*"

With a clunk the recording comes to an end. We stand side by side in silence for a while, trying to absorb the implications of what we've just been told.

"What do you think he means by the *Guardians*?"

"I've no idea," Raphael says wearily.

I push the machine to one side as instructed and underneath find a small trapdoor no bigger than a hatbox lid. I lift it up and find a cavity below with a handle at the bottom.

And I do as I was told. I don't know what else to do.

I grip the handle with two hands and pull it with all my strength. It releases with a clunk.

I hear a crash from somewhere in the house.

And then a scream.

Mother.

Chapter Twenty-Nine

We jump on to the zip and shoot up to the top of the house, the cherub clinging to Raphael's shirtsleeve, her toes tucked into his belt. What have I done? Have I hurt Mother? Has Strix attacked her?

"Could he have found his way back in?" I cry.

"But why would he be attacking *her*? Isn't he here for me?"

The zip comes to a halt and we leap into the corridor.

Fledgling

I right myself just in time to avoid crashing into Mother, who is standing at the bottom of her spiral staircase with her back to us.

"Mama!" I cry. "What's happened? Are you hurt?" The smell of almonds hangs heavily in the air, and I glance at Raphael, worried his wounds are oozing again. Mother is looking at something on the stairs, her head in her hands. Her hair is wild, as if she has had an electrical shock – but she is clearly not being attacked.

I grab her arm and spin her to face me. She is shaking. But then I see what she is staring at. "Mother," I say, suddenly raging. "I thought something terrible had happened!"

"Something terrible *has* happened, Cassie," she says, breathing in and out deeply through pursed lips. "Look—" She points at a little pile of fur on the stairs. It's a dead rat lying on its back with its back legs crossed and its front paws tucked behind its head, as if sunbathing. It's wearing a little black top hat and a pair of red-velvet trousers.

What is she doing dragging me up here for this?

"Mama, it's just a joke," I say. "It must be one of Papa's. Look, it's even got Papa's trademark stitching."

"If this was meant as a joke, I do not find it very funny," she says, unable to draw her eyes from the creature. But then her mood suddenly changes, and a look flits across her face, something closer to fear than anger. "Get it out of the house now, Cassie," she says darkly, as if the rat is an unexploded bomb. She takes a deep breath, smooths her dress and pats her hair. "And where is your father? I wish to tell him I am not amused."

I shrug. He won't have meant to upset Mother. He probably left it as a gift, like Bram when he's in trouble.

Mother suddenly notices Raphael. "Oh," she says. "It's you." There is a slight edge to her voice. Did I imagine her eyes settling on the cherub, now perched on his shoulder, for just a second, before flicking away?

"Hello, Frau Engel," he says. "Would you like me to help you with the rat?"

I glare at him, trying to make eye contact, inclining my head towards the zip, to remind him we have other things to do, but he's too taken with the rat to notice.

"If you would," Mother says, waving a pale hand towards it. She shivers. "Has someone left a window open?" She glances about the corridor as a gust of icy air slips past us. We must have left the owlery door open in our rush to reach Mother.

Raphael kneels in front of the rat, picks it up and cradles it in his arms like a baby. "It's rather sweet," he says, rubbing its slightly swollen belly. "Would you mind if I keep it, Frau Engel?"

Mother looks at him, eyebrows raised in astonishment. "Well, if dead rats are your thing, dear, be my guest. So long as I never see it again, I really don't care what you do with it."

Raphael looks pleased, and scratches the rat behind an ear. "I shall call him Rufus," he announces. "Rufus the Rat."

We need to get down to the engine room, but I also have to ask about Emaline. I check she isn't within earshot.

"Mother, I have a quick question for you."

"So long as it's not about the blasted owlery."

"No, no, it isn't. It's about Emaline."

"What about Emaline?" She looks bored already. "Is she planning something frightful for supper? Is that it? Is she boiling eels in the kitchen as we speak?"

"No, it's not that. I was just wondering how much you know about her."

"What do you mean? What she likes for breakfast? What she does on her days off?"

"No," I snap. "I'm wondering how long she's been here. How long she's worked for us."

"Oh, I don't know, darling. She's part of the furniture – like one of the old wardrobes."

227

"But does she have family?" I say impatiently. "Where does she go on her days off?"

"I haven't a clue, Cassie. Emaline's movements are none of my business."

I wonder if she's embarrassed not to know this, as she suddenly appears a little contrite. I want to shout at her. How can she not know? We practically live with the woman. She knows everything about us, but we clearly know nothing about her.

Mother must have spotted the expression on my face, as she starts to bluster.

"It's not something I've spent much time thinking about. I do have a life and a career, you know. And I have to rehearse. And run this ridiculous house. And look after you, and pander to your whims."

"My whims?" I spit. "What whims, Mother, do you spend so much time pandering to?"

Raphael shuffles awkwardly next to me and finally starts to move nearer the zip.

"Oh, I don't know. That business with the cape, that sort of thing." She's edging towards the music-room stairs now.

"What business with the cape?" I say, also stepping towards the zip, regretting starting this conversation.

"Oh, you know, when your father bought you that

ridiculously expensive cape."

Of course this is what she does. When a conversation becomes tricky or heated, she goes on the attack or changes the subject.

"So, we don't know anything about Emaline," I say.

"It appears perhaps we don't, darling," Mother says. She turns away from me, clips up her spiral staircase to the music room, and slams the door behind her.

I look at Raphael, cringing. He smiles at me. "It's all right," he says. "I know what she's like. She's probably just a little out of sorts after the fright with the rat."

I wish I could forgive her so easily.

Chapter Thirty

The doorbell rings. The sudden peal of bells in the silent house makes my heart skip a beat.

The cherub is agitated and flaps about our heads like a giant fly.

The doorbell rings again.

"Will someone answer the blooming door!" Papa shouts from somewhere else in the house.

"I think you should go to my room," I say to Raphael.

"I'll send whoever it is away."

I jump on to the zip, not caring much as I practically free-fall to the ground floor. I pump on the foot brake just before the platform reaches the hall flagstones.

I heave the door open, and find Crunch and Grind on the doorstep.

"Hello?" I say, wondering if they were due to pay Grandma a visit today or have news of Frau Fischer. We stand facing each other for a few moments.

"We are here to see Frau Engel," they say in unison.

"I don't think she's expecting you." I can't put my finger on it, but something about the way their eyes slide from side to side makes them appear a little shifty.

One of the nurses pulls out a battered leather notebook from her satchel, licks a finger, and slowly and methodically flicks through the pages, while I tap my foot impatiently on the floor. The pony snorts behind her, sending plumes of hot breath into the icy air. A deep frown is etched across her forehead, but finally she finds the page she's looking for. "Your maid. Emaline. She sent us a message," she says.

I look at them in astonishment. "Emaline sent you a message?"

"Ja," says the other. "She says Frau Engel is hallucinating. She is concerned about *that* pump." She spits on to the little pile of rocks to the side of the door and they look at each other shiftily again. She slams the book closed and returns it to her satchel.

"I've just been to see her," I lie, certain they're lying too, "and she seemed much the same as normal." Emaline wouldn't have called for them without checking with us first. "I'm sorry you've had a wasted journey." I start to close the door, but a fat boot flies towards me and wedges it open.

"We think Frau Engel would appreciate a visit," the owner of the boot says, her eyes inches from mine.

I don't know what to do. They're the last people I need crashing about the house with everything going on. I try to push the door closed again. "I'm so sorry, but we're very busy at the moment. Could you come back tomorrow?"

Crunch or Grind continues her pressure on the door, forcing it open, sliding me back into the hallway. Eventually I give up; she's twice as strong as me. "I'm sure she would love to see you," I say, stepping away from the door, swearing at myself under my breath.

As we walk past the zip towards the stairs, they glance at the platform. It's hovering expectantly, waiting for its next passenger. "Would you like to use that, rather than the stairs?" I say, waving my hand towards it, glancing back at the engine-room door. A strange metallic smell seems to coming from it.

"Ja, that would beneficial."

They jostle each other for space on the platform while I quickly generate the steam for the cannon.

"And how is Frau Fischer?" I say. "Has she settled in?"

"She is well," one says.

"Ja, they say she is eating a lot," says the other.

When they are ready, I release the lever and wait for a minute or so until they have risen through the ceiling. I run up the stairs after them.

I meet them in my corridor. Mother is barring their way. "May I help you?" she says, looking up at them imperiously. They are even taller than her, and each twice as wide. I can see she is a little intimidated.

"Mother! They are here to see to Grandma."

"Why? Haven't they already visited her this week?"

"Yes they have, but there's a problem with the pump, apparently, that needs looking at."

"Oh, well, if that's the case…" She steps aside to let them pass.

Crunch and Grind stomp down the corridor towards Grandma's room, muttering to each other. Old portraits and bony heads tremble on their hangings as they pass.

Mother and I face each other awkwardly. It seems that events are conspiring to stop me getting to the engine room.

Mother looks like she wishes to talk. "Now, how are *you*, darling?" She taps my arm with her fingertips. "You mustn't worry about Grandma."

"I'm not worrying about her at the moment," I say stiffly.

She smiles at me. "You know she's preparing to leave. We do have to be ready for that."

Why does she have to choose *this* moment to discuss Grandma? I hate talking about Grandma dying, and certainly don't want to right now, with everything else going on.

I'm relieved to hear shuffling footsteps behind me. It's Papa.

Mother's mood changes. She glares at him. "I did not appreciate the rat," she hisses.

"What rat is that, dear?"

I look out of the window. The clouds are now stacked one above the other. The sight reminds me of the anvil-shaped clouds in the illuminated manuscript. I shiver and turn away.

"The rat you so charmingly left on my staircase."

Papa looks at her blankly.

"The rat in the top hat," she says slowly, as if talking to an idiot.

"What *are* you talking about, Gabriele?"

"Oh, don't look at me with those innocent eyes. I know exactly what you're up to."

"Gabriele, my dear, I would love to help you, but I know absolutely nothing about a rat."

Mother narrows her eyes.

I back away down the corridor. They barely speak to each other. Why are they doing this now?

"Cassie!" Mother barks. "Tell your father about the rat. He seems to think I'm making it up."

"There was a rat on Mother's staircase, Papa," I say. "We guessed it was one of your jokes as it was wearing a top hat."

Papa stares at me with wide watery eyes and I wonder if he has been drinking. He turns to face Mother. "Well, your rat sounds like a fine fellow, dearest, but he is absolutely nothing to do with me."

Mother looks worried. "Well, if *you* didn't put it there, then who did?" She juts her chin out and glares at him.

"I have absolutely no idea." He looks almost offended. "*You* of all people should know that I don't do rats."

"I have no idea what you *do* do these days, dear. If you'll stuff a cat, then why not a rat?"

235

"Rats are horrid creatures, Gabriele. Why on earth would I wish to preserve one?" He pauses. "And anyway, they're ruddy awful things to stuff. Far too fiddly."

"Don't swear in front of Cassie!"

"Why not? You swear in front of her all the time."

"I do not!"

It's time to go. I slip away to find Raphael, wondering who left the rat on the stairs. Clearly not Grandma. And definitely not Mother. And if Papa didn't put it there, that only leaves one person.

But why would Emaline leave a rat in a top hat on Mother's staircase?

Chapter Thirty-One

I run down to my room and find Raphael curled up on the floor of my bedroom, his head in his hands, the cherub by his side. "Is it happening again?" I say, rushing in and falling to my knees by his side. I'd hoped it would be weeks, or even months, before his wings started growing again. "Would you like me to take your bindings off?"

He shakes his head. "No, it's passing now. And it's

nothing like last time."

A rumble of thunder shakes the house. I open the window and peer out. A light drizzle has settled over us, and in the dark the sheer face of our rock is grim and foreboding. Another burst of thunder shakes the house and I grip the windowsill to steady myself. I slam the window and pull the curtain across.

A grinding metallic sound fills the room, and the floor vibrates.

"What was that?" I whisper.

Raphael looks alarmed. "It felt like it was coming from lower down in the house."

"It must be the engine room," I say. "We were told to go straight there, Raphael! I should have just ignored Mother." I try to sound more confident than I feel. "I'll go. You don't need to come too."

"Yes I do," he says, heaving himself up from the floor. "You can't go there on your own!" He glances at the cherub. "And she should come too. She's proving to be quite useful."

I nod, relieved he's being so insistent. "But what about your back?"

"My back is feeling better already."

I'm not convinced but I don't argue.

★

I open the engine-room door cautiously. A blast of steam hits me in the face, making me leap backwards. I have never known the room to generate so much vapour. It could be a problem with the boiler or the steam cannon – but the zip was working perfectly well just now, suggesting both are in order. This must be something to do with me pulling the lever in the library. We back out for a moment, allowing steam to billow past us before stepping inside.

Everything in here is shrouded in a cloak of dirty yellow fog, making it difficult to see anything other than the ancient boiler glowing moodily in the corner. It's gloomy in here at the best of times, with only a cracked oil lamp to light the room, but now I can't even see two feet ahead of me. The sharp tang of oil and rusting metal hangs heavily in the air. I turn to check that Raphael and the cherub are still close.

Grandpa taught me that if there's ever a problem in the engine room, the first thing to do is check the controls. I feel my way through the murk, stepping carefully towards the bank of dials that monitor our heating and hot water. I wipe condensation from their glass fronts with my sleeve and peer at them. The gold needles within the little boxes are pointing to the correct readings. The mechanism for Mother's roof is also properly set.

With the engine-room door still open the air slowly clears, and I notice that the far wall, a riveted iron screen, has completely disappeared, revealing the bare rock from which the room was carved so long ago. Lengths of rusting chain stretch across its sheer face, twisting and weaving round a network of metal cogs, like a giant cobweb. In the centre is a large lever. The peeling paint, still clinging to it in places, suggests it was once a vibrant red.

I look up and see a long slot in the ceiling with a line of grey metal running along it. I realise that the old steel wall must have slid up into the slot, revealing this complex mechanism hidden behind it.

"The whole wall has lifted away," I whisper.

Raphael examines the chains. "There must be some sort of cable connecting the owlery to the engine room," he says, running his fingers along the rusty links. "And I wonder what this network of chains is for. They've obviously been here for some time." He taps the newly revealed stone, as if checking it's solid, and peers up into the void above. "Has this happened before?"

"No, never. I thought the metal wall was just cladding, to keep out moisture from the rock. It never occurred to me there would be anything behind it."

I notice a faded note held in place by a split pin above the lever. I grab it and turn it over. But as I angle it towards the light I groan. Whatever was once written here is no longer legible; faded blue ink has travelled senselessly across the page. I touch the cold rock and rub my fingers together. It is damp.

My eyes are drawn to the lever in the middle of the wall. It seems too obvious to pull it.

"Perhaps the note contained a warning not to touch it," Raphael says.

"But then why have it, if it isn't to be touched?" I have learned over the years not to fiddle with anything in the house unless I'm certain I know its intended purpose, but something tells me this is here for a reason – a reason I shouldn't ignore.

"I think we should pull it," I say.

I take the lever in both hands and pull it down until it clunks into position. This *must* be what my great-great-grandfather intended.

Initially nothing happens. We look around the room nervously. The room begins to shake, the expanse of chain starts to quiver, and the cogs judder into life. I grab Raphael's arm, already worrying I've done the wrong thing. The cogs slowly begin to turn, dragging the rusting chains through them, until eventually the whole wall is alive with metal chains, like a nest of snakes. A deafening metallic sound fills the air.

I run out into the hall and look around. What have I done?

It is darker than usual in the hallway, with just a narrow shaft of light coming in through the small window by the front door. An iron grille has fallen across it! I open the front door and find a six-foot grille stretched across the doorway like a portcullis. I shake the metalwork. It is solid and unmoving.

I realise that no one can get into our house.

But equally no one will be able to get out, including Crunch and Grind.

We are trapped.

Chapter Thirty-Two

Mother is calling from somewhere upstairs. She sounds frightened.

Raphael opens the window by the door as far is it will go, reaches out and rattles the grille. A blast of icy air hits him in the face. He slams it closed and blows on his hands. "Do you think they're at every window?"

"Judging by the noise when they came down, I think they might be," I say. I bite my lip and glance outside.

"My great-great-grandfather must have designed this to protect us," I say. "How dangerous *are* these creatures?"

Raphael shakes his head, but says nothing.

Mother calls again and I groan. "How am I going to explain all this?" I say, waving at the window. "She's going to be furious."

"You didn't have a choice, Cassie. And I'll come with you." Raphael glances up at the cherub darting around about a foot above his head. He reaches up and catches her by an ankle and pulls her into his arms. "Sorry, you need to come too," he says.

"I'll just explain about the grilles for now," I say.

"You have to tell her about everything, Cassie." His eyes are still the brightest blue, but he looks terrified and deathly pale. I can't believe it's his time to rise.

"But she'll never believe me," I say.

"I think you have to. About me too. And the cherub." He glances outside. "And the Sturmfalken. We're going to need your parents' help."

I nod glumly, knowing I don't really have a choice.

★

We find them at the bottom of the music-room steps, examining the grille across the opposite window. Mother's hands are shaking and a vein is protruding at her temple. She pounces as soon as we jump off the zip.

"Cassie, what have you done?"

"I need to speak with you both," I say, checking Raphael is still close behind me. Papa is wringing his hands. I wish I could protect him from this.

The cherub breaks free from Raphael's grip, flies to the window and peers outside. She seems as agitated as Mother. Papa seems oblivious to her and Mother looks too frightened to focus on anything.

"We found a hidden wall in the engine room," I say, deciding to give them as little information as possible. "There was a lever in there, which I pulled. And I believe it caused these grilles to slot into place at the windows."

"And are you able to unpull the lever, should you wish to do so?" Mother says.

"I'm not sure," I reply, "but I think we need to leave them where they are for now."

Papa turns to Mother. "Did you know our house had hidden ironwork, dear?"

"No, but the house is full of surprises," she says. "It's probably just another of my great-grandfather's gimmicks."

A crash of thunder shakes the house and we are briefly plunged into darkness. It's too early to be so dark.

A sudden movement outside catches my eye.

I scream.

A Sturmfalke is heading towards us at speed. It doesn't appear to be slowing down. It hits the grille with a sickening crunch, its beak splintering on the grille. It falls to its death on the rock far below.

I force myself to look out of the window. The air outside is thick with Sturmfalken. There must be hundreds of them out there, circling the house above a layer of low-lying cloud that has wrapped round our rock like candyfloss. Our plight will be invisible to anyone in Edenburg.

Papa looks over my shoulder. "Cassie," he says quietly, "do you know what is happening?"

"I think they might be Sturmfalken," I say.

He looks at me blankly. "Sturm what?"

"They're a type of bird, Papa. I think they're trying to get in, which is why we need these grilles."

We leap away from the window as another one approaches at speed. It crashes into the grille and falls from view.

Papa looks at Mother. "Do you know anything about this, dear?"

She doesn't reply. She is too busy staring at Raphael. "Are you quite well, boy?" she says. "You look like you've seen a ghost."

He has sunk to his knees in agony.

"Please do something to help him," I urge the cherub. "Do what you did last time."

"Who are you talking to?" Papa says, glancing in the cherub's direction.

"Um, it's a little difficult to explain…"

★

Mother and Papa listen in silence as I tell them what Raphael is, and how wings are growing from his shoulder blades. I tell them about Strix too. And about the Sturmfalken attack in the middle of the night. And the gramophone recording.

When I finish speaking, I look up at them. They are staring at me, their eyes wide.

Papa looks at Raphael but says nothing. Mother turns and flees up to the music room, and slams the door behind her.

Raphael is on his knees in pain. I wish I knew how to help him.

Papa comes to me and wraps me in his arms. "Why didn't you tell us about all this sooner? Why didn't you ask for help?" He holds me at arm's length. "I guess you think I'm pretty useless."

"I thought you wouldn't believe me," I say, fighting back tears. "And you have enough going on with … you know, after everything that happened."

He looks for a moment as if he might cry. "Still, you should have asked."

I wish he didn't look so hurt.

He turns to Raphael. "You poor, poor boy. Are you in pain now?"

"It's passing," Raphael says. He looks like he is burning with a fever. "It comes in waves."

"There's something else," I say, glancing up towards the music room, wondering if Mother will come back down. "There's someone else here – well, *something* else."

"What sort of something?" says Papa, glancing around nervously.

"A sort of angel," I say eventually. "A cherub, to be more precise."

Papa runs a hand through his already dishevelled hair. "So, we have a boy turning into an angel in front of our eyes. And now a cherub! Where is it?"

"Not everyone can see her," I say. "She decides who can and can't see her."

"Can I touch her if I can't see her?"

I shake my head. "She's over there." I nod to where she is hovering above Raphael's shoulder.

Papa doesn't look convinced. "Your mind might be playing tricks on you, darling, what with everything else going on." The cherub lands on Raphael's shoulder and fixes Papa with a cold stare. "I see all sorts of things that aren't there."

"But that's after a bottle of schnapps," I say. I regret it as soon as the words have left my mouth.

He nods. "You're right. I know that. But I do see strange things when I'm sober too."

His eyes suddenly gleam, and he steps towards Raphael as if roused by such an exciting possibility. "A cherub and a boy angel! Cassie, do you realise what this means? A discovery such as this could make our fortune! The greatest scientists in the world would wish to examine such creatures." He looks around. "So where is the cherub?"

"You are not stuffing the cherub," I say through gritted teeth. "How could you say such a thing?"

He looks horrified. "What do you take me for, Cassie? Of course I wouldn't stuff it. I just think people would be interested. They'd pay good money to see it." He glances at Raphael and I wonder if he'd like to turn Raphael into some sort of exhibit too.

Where is Emaline? And what about Crunch and Grind? Surely they must have been disturbed by the noise of the grilles falling. I'm just about to head down to Grandma's room to investigate when the cherub lifts up from Raphael's shoulder and flies at speed up the narrow staircase towards the music room.

For just a second, we stand like statues, none of us daring to move. The cherub reaches the closed music room door and then flies back down to us, and back up to the door again, as if instructing us to follow her. She's making the most peculiar noise, like an animal in pain. I race up the steps towards her, with Raphael and Papa close behind.

Chapter Thirty-Three

We burst into the music room. Mother is sitting, bent over, on the chaise longue, her face in her hands.

It is often colder up here than in the rest of the house, but I don't think it's ever been like this. I kick the central-heating pipe and run my hand along the radiator like Grandpa used to do. It's ice-cold. I check the windows. They are closed, but I realise with a sinking heart that there are no metal grilles protecting them. Mother added this room years after the rest of the house was built. Of course she wouldn't have thought to install hidden iron bars at the windows. Outside the sky is black, the moon lost behind angry, turbulent clouds.

Papa presses his nose to one of the window's small leaded panes. "They're still out there," he says, turning to face us, his features grey and craggy. Mother rises from the chaise longue, crow-like in her long black cloak, and walks unsteadily towards us. She peers over Papa's shoulder. I run to another window and look out, allowing my eyes to adjust to the gloom. Bright talons scrape against the glass and I scream.

"Cassie!" Mother cries. "Was it another one?"

"Yes," I say. I glance out again. "But I think it's gone now."

The creatures are here for Raphael; I know that. Like they came for my great-great-uncle, Ramiel. They want to kill the angel before it rises, while they still can.

Raphael joins us at the window and I glance surreptitiously at his back. I'm certain his wings haven't grown any more. Can it really be his time? Surely he has to learn to fly before he can rise. I can't believe he's ready for this. He's like a furnace as always, and I slide a little closer to him to absorb some of his warmth. He turns to me and smiles anxiously.

I run round the room and slam the shutters closed, but I have no idea if they'll be strong enough to keep a Sturmfalke out.

A fresh blast of icy air from above hits me in the face.

I look up. "The roof's opening!" I scream.

We stand and watch in horror as the vast panels above us begin to separate. Soon the music room will be open to the night sky like a moonflower.

Through the narrow gaps between the panels I can just make out the steady beat of wings, and a sea of bright, hungry eyes.

Raphael looks up and swallows. "There are hundreds out there," he says, his eyes wide with fear.

They shriek and squabble, bickering like siblings before dinner has even begun.

How can the roof be opening? It never opens without someone setting the mechanism in the engine room. And we're all here.

"I need to go to the engine room," I shout over the noise of the wind and the screeching of the birds. I pray I have time to close the roof before the panels are sufficiently open to let the creatures in. I hope I won't be too late.

A crash of thunder rattles the house. A second later, a flash of lightning filters in through the narrow gaps in the shutters, illuminating Mother and Papa's lead-white faces. My stomach lurches as the house pitches briefly towards the forest, before righting itself again.

The cherub lands on my shoulder, and with her hot breath in my ear, I feel strangely calm. The gaps between each of the roof sections are now as wide as a fist. I pass the cherub to Raphael. I don't wait to see if he wants to come too. I should only be a few minutes.

I race down the spiral staircase, two steps at a time, jump on to the zip and fly down to the engine room.

I throw the door open and find Emaline leaning over the controls of the roof mechanism.

"Emaline!" I scream. "What are you doing? Have you not seen what's happening outside?"

She appears not to hear me.

"Emaline," I cry again, rushing to her. "We have to close the roof!"

She nudges me away with a broad shoulder.

"Emaline!" I shout. "We're being attacked!"

I try to pull her hands away from the controls but she is too heavy. I grab one of her thick leathery arms and tug at it, but she shakes me off.

"Emaline!" I shout again, desperate to make eye contact. "We have to shut the roof." I pull at her sleeve and she spins to face me, seizes me by my upper arms, lifts me off my feet and hurls me across the room. I skid across the floor and crash into the side of the boiler.

I leap up, raging, and throw myself at her and cling to her back, reaching over her shoulder to grab the lever of the roof mechanism, but she bucks like a horse. I can't hold on any longer and tumble to the floor, landing painfully on my hip. But before I can jump up again, she throws herself on top of me, pinning me to the floor, her face inches from mine. Sweat from her forehead falls to my cheeks and trickles behind my ears.

My head spins as the weight of her body takes my breath away. She grabs my neck and presses her thumbs into my windpipe. I gag and pressure builds in my eyes so much I fear they might explode.

I try to scream but I cannot make a sound. I don't know how long I have been down here now. The roof will have opened even more now. Will it be enough to let the Sturmfalken in?

Emaline presses harder, and I drift in and out of consciousness, gasping for breath.

Suddenly I hear a crash, and through swollen eyes I see two blurry shapes rush into the room. The pressure on my throat is released as Emaline is dragged off me and thrown to the floor, her head hitting the flagstones with a crunch. Then two muscle-bound bodies leap on top of her. She thrashes, trying to fight them off, but her attackers are too strong.

I ease myself up painfully and limp towards the roof mechanism, blinking as the room comes into focus. It's Crunch and Grind.

"Tie her up," one of the nurses orders the other, pointing to a coil of rope on the workbench. "That should hold her for now."

They wrap Emaline up like a chrysalis and lash her to a large cog above her head. She swears at them as she tries to break free of her bindings.

My arms throb where Emaline grabbed them, and my head thumps. Through a haze of pain I remember I have to close the roof. My hands shake as I try to push the mechanism into place, but it's jammed. I kick the lever. It won't budge.

"I need help!" I scream, ignoring the fire engulfing my throat. "I have to close the roof. There are creatures. Above the house! Trying to get in! *She* did this. I can't close it. Something's jamming it."

One of the nurses grips the lever hard and pulls. But it won't budge. The other joins her, but even together they cannot move it. I spot a metal bar wedged within the bowels of the machine. I can't reach it.

"We need to get back up there," I cry. "Everyone is

in the music room and the sky is full of—" I don't have time to explain all this. "We have to get back up there now."

I have never seen Crunch and Grind move so fast. We don't stop to discuss Emaline and what possessed her to do something so terrible. The grandfather clock chimes eight times. On a normal evening she would be preparing to serve dinner.

I pump the lever frantically to release the steam for the zip, and we climb on, shuffling to make space for each other on the platform. I end up squashed between Crunch and Grind and I reach out and press the red button. Already I wish I had taken the stairs, but once we start rising it's too late. I almost scream in frustration at the sluggish rate of our ascent. My head is jammed into a large bosom, and its owner's heart is pounding even faster than mine. I cannot imagine Crunch or Grind being frightened of anything. They seem so invincible.

Shots ring out from above us. I know Papa still has a pistol from his army days. What is he doing with it?

We finally reach the top floor. I leap off the zip and race towards the spiral staircase that leads up to the music room, with Crunch and Grind just behind me.

The roof is wide open and the Sturmfalken are beating their wings high above us, their beady eyes watching everyone carefully.

Raphael rushes to us. "Where have you been? I was so worried about you!"

"Emaline was opening the roof," I cry, explaining briefly what happened. I look around the room in horror. "There are so many, Raphael. How can we stop them coming in?"

"I don't think we can," he says.

"Has the cherub done anything?"

"No, she's been like that the whole time." He points towards the mahogany chiffonier, above which the cherub is hovering in mid-air, watching the swirling mass above her.

"Have they hurt you?"

"No, they haven't attacked me. They've just been swooping down at us and then retreating out of reach. They haven't hurt anyone. It's as if they're waiting for something."

Mother is standing in the middle of the room, her eyes wild, her hair dishevelled, holding her arms over her head as the creatures gather above her like a storm cloud. They swoop down towards her and peck at her hair and clothes.

Papa is leaping around the room, shooting up wildly with his old pistol. Occasionally a creature falls to its death at Mother's feet.

Icy rain streams into the room. Rumbles of thunder shake the house, and flashes of lightning briefly illuminate the sea of terrified faces around me. Crunch and Grind stand side by side, their fists balled, preparing to fight.

I hear a shriek from above and look up to see a creature far larger than the Sturmfalken around us. It is the creature from the owlery.

Strix.

He hovers above us, the steady beat of his wings seeming to silence everything in the room. Even the storm appears to still for just a moment.

He shrieks again and the Sturmfalken fly up, gathering around him like a swarm of hornets.

We are all still, as if life has been momentarily paused. Hundreds of eyes watch us.

"We have to get out of here!" I scream.

"Leave me," Mother shouts. "I'll deal with this."

"You can't deal with this on your own," I cry, running to her. "How can you deal with all this?" I wave my arms up at the flock of Sturmfalken above us.

"They'll only break down the door and follow you if you flee," she says. "We need someone up here to keep them at bay."

Papa runs to her side. "But you can't do that on your own, Gabriele."

"Just go!" she hisses. "I'm staying here."

"I'm not leaving you, Mama," I say.

"I'll be perfectly fine, Cassie. I've dealt with far worse than this at the opera house."

"And I'm not leaving you either," says Papa.

Strix screeches again and, before we can say another word, the Sturmfalken shoot down towards us.

They are organised now and deadly. It is too late to escape.

The birds head straight for Raphael and then Mother. I run to her, screaming and swatting at the creatures until my lungs feel as if they might burst.

Then the air in the room changes. The cherub rises above us, her eyes on fire, immersing Mother, Raphael and me in a sea of luminescence. The sense of pressure on my body is familiar to me, but Mother stares at me, her eyes wide with fear. I turn to her, my arms outstretched. She reaches towards me and our fingertips touch. I take her hands in mine and draw her to me. Raphael wades to us, and we take his hands too. I force the dense liquid air surrounding us in and out of my lungs.

Papa has discarded his pistol and is now swiping at

Sturmfalken with his walking stick. I scream soundlessly when I see them tearing at him with their talons, ripping his face and his hands as he tries to protect himself. I try to fight my way out of the luminescence, but it sucks me back in. I watch in despair as Papa is beset by Sturmfalken.

A roar like a battle cry fills the room. It is Crunch and Grind, raging and crashing about like a couple of bulls, grabbing Sturmfalken and smashing them against the walls.

A pair of Sturmfalken flies at one of the nurses. She catches them by their feet and smashes them together like a pair of cymbals. They tumble to their death, shrieking and writhing, eyeballs dangling from empty sockets.

And then something happens with the luminescence, as if the air that has been protecting us is melting. I look desperately to the cherub for help.

I realise the Sturmfalken are now attacking her. She is overwhelmed.

I break free from Mother and Raphael and rush to the cherub, screaming. I tear at the creatures with my hands, but they surround me, pecking at my hair and face, and I am suddenly lost in a cloud of claws, rotten breath and beating wings. Raphael runs to me, ripping the creatures away. He tries to wrap his arms protectively round me, but I wriggle away. I am supposed to be protecting him! I grab the nearest bird and slam it into the floorboards, wincing as its neck snaps in two with a crack.

And then they turn on Raphael.

I roar like a wild boar. They cannot hurt Raphael! I thrash at them wildly, desperate and out of control. Mother rushes towards me and pulls me away from him. She takes my hands in hers, her nails sinking into my palms.

I cry out in pain. "What are you doing?" I cry.

"We need to sing!" she shouts.

I look at her as if she is mad, and try to twist free from her grip.

"Sing, Cassie," she repeats, more calmly this time.

"But I cannot sing – you know that!" I hiss.

She pulls me to face her. "You can, Cassie. And we need to sing together. Now!"

Grandma's words echo in my head and I remember how I screamed in the forest. And in the owlery. Something happened then that I couldn't make sense of at the time. Were my screams powerful enough to inadvertently shatter the glass display case? I killed the Sturmfalke in the forest. Raphael had buried a pile of splintered bloody glass and feathers. Was that how I had killed the creature? With my voice?

And so I sing. Papa puts his hands over his ears. Even Crunch and Grind stop their killing for just a second.

Mama and I sing together in a rising arpeggio, until we can sing no higher.

Around us, as if time has slowed, Papa and Raphael continue their fight against the Sturmfalken, working together, protecting each other, slaying the creatures despite their wounds – keeping them away from Mother and me. Crunch and Grind form a protective shield round the cherub. She looks weak and broken, like when she first landed on my bed.

A Sturmfalke flies straight towards us, above Papa's reach, its eyes crazed and desperate-looking. But just as it reaches us, it explodes mid-air. Glass fragments shower down on us and it falls in a tangled heap of feathers at our feet. And then another comes. And another. Mother and I breathe in and sing again. One by one they fly at us, and one by one they explode before they reach us, landing in heaps of fractured talons, stinking intestines and glass bone fragments. I don't know how long we sing like this. It seems to last forever, but also no time at all.

We sing until the last one has fallen.

★

My throat is on fire and my lungs burn. The floor is awash with blood-soaked glass and the remains of dead Sturmfalken. Papa leans against the wall, deep wounds on his face bleeding profusely. Raphael is slumped on the floor. Crunch or Grind rolls down one of her stockings and moves towards Papa. A look of horror briefly crosses his face before he allows her to wrap it round his head.

Mother begins to hum, and I glance at her in irritation. But then I remember how she hums to lubricate her vocal cords. I copy her, and find the soft vibration helps to douse the flames in my throat.

A furious shriek above us makes me jump.

Strix.

He is still alive. He swoops above us, circling the room, surveying his decimated army. I remind myself that his eyesight is poor and pray no one moves. But Crunch and Grind run at him and leap to catch him. He dodges them, and with two swift flicks of his tail sends them flying across the room.

Papa runs from the room and disappears down the spiral staircase.

Mother squeezes my hand and looks at me with her eyebrows raised. I nod. And so together we sing through our pain. Heads held high, tonight we are the Queen of the Night and her daughter.

Strix thrashes his tail, but he does not explode. We sing louder and higher, but our voices are too weak. He dives towards us, shrieking, as if laughing in our faces. Mocking us.

Papa bursts into the room and runs towards us. He is carrying the bellows from the dining room.

"Papa?" I cry.

He runs at Strix, screaming.

Strix swivels to face him and hovers, his face inches from Papa's. He shrieks into Papa's face.

"Papa, no!" I howl, rushing towards him.

"Stay away, Cassie!" he shouts.

I step back from them both, my heart racing.

Papa plunges the paddles of the bellows together and sprays a cloud of white powder into Strix's face.

Strix inhales. Within seconds he is screeching and thrashing, his body convulsing as if he's in agony. Yellow foam sprays from his beak, and I duck to avoid being drenched in the foul-smelling liquid. He seems to be struggling to fly now, and one side of his body dips towards the floor.

He screams in frustration and pain, before turning sharply upwards and disappearing into the night.

The room falls silent.

We all look at Papa.

"What was in the bellows?" I say.

"Arsenic!" he says, looking rather pleased with himself.

★

The storm is passing, revealing bright stars above.

"Thank you," I say to Crunch and Grind.

"Just doing our job," one says, drawing me into her arms and rubbing the top of my head with her knuckles. The other opens a window, and together they begin to toss dead Sturmfalken out into the night. As the broken creatures bounce down the rock face, they make a tinkling sound – like glass shattering into tiny fragments.

"That'll be a warning to any more out there," they say grimly.

★

The moon emerges from behind the retreating clouds, lighting the sky like a beacon. Mother looks up and swallows. She keeps glancing up. Does she know what is about to happen to Raphael?

"Have they fully unfurled?" I whisper to him, noticing how hunched he is looking.

"I don't know," he says fearfully. "I don't think so."

"I'm sure we would know if it was time," I say. "You

cannot rise until your wings are fully grown."

"But then what was all this about?" he says, waving his arms. "They wouldn't have come like that unless it was time."

"You cannot leave me!" I wail.

Raphael shakes his head. "I don't want to leave you either, Cassie."

"He's not ready to go!" I scream at the cherub, perched on a pile of vocal scores on the chiffonier. "He's too young! Can't you see that?" I run to her. "You must stop this. There must be another way."

I look at Raphael. "You could just refuse to go. She can't make you!"

Raphael glances up to the night sky. The storm is passing, revealing a thousand bright stars far above.

"Please don't take him," I cry again. "He isn't ready!"

"We all know that, Cassie. He is just a boy. Of course he's not ready." It is Mother.

The cherub stretches her wings, lifts into the air and flies to her.

Mother takes her in her arms.

"What do you mean?" I say, my eyes flicking between Mother and the cherub. "Mama?"

"He's too young, Cassie. He still has much to learn. It's me she has come for."

I look at her in horror, and my legs give way. I sink to my knees. She unties the ribbon round her neck and lets her cloak fall to the floor. Crunch and Grind step towards her, almost as if they were expecting this. As if this was all planned. And then Mother lights up from the inside, like Raphael the night his wings began to unfurl – and the cherub that night in my room. Mother's eyes don't leave me as she reaches for something over her shoulder. She unhooks a clasp at the back of her dress. She takes a deep breath, and slowly two wings unfurl. Vast adult angel wings. They are beautiful but terrifying too.

"No!" I scream.

Not her. Not Mother.

"Mama, no! You are my mother! You are not an angel!"

Father is as white as death. "Gabriele?"

"I am sorry, my darling," she says. "I couldn't tell you. I hoped this day would never come."

Papa claps a hand to his mouth, seemingly unable to believe what his eyes are telling him. He sinks to the floor, curls into a ball, covering his ears. I run to him and wrap my arms round him. "How could you not tell us?" I shout at her. "How long have you known?" I kiss the top of Papa's stockinged head. "Did you not think to tell

Papa? Or me? Your daughter?"

"I didn't tell you because I didn't know when or if I would have to go," she cries. "I didn't tell you because I prayed this would never happen. That it would go away if I ignored it." She crouches next to me and touches my arm. "It has been so difficult to conceal my wings," she says. "I had to keep you both away from me. To protect you."

She looks at my expression. "I was just trying to protect you, Cassie!"

"But you didn't protect me!" I shout. "How did you protect me? By making yourself cold and horrible and distant?" I am in such a rage I almost spit the words in her face. How could she keep this from us? "You are my mama!" I say quietly. "You should have told me."

And then I notice the tears running down her cheeks. I throw my arms round her and she wraps hers round me. I breathe her in, desperate to never let her go. Maybe she couldn't tell us. How do you tell someone you are going to leave them forever? That you are not what they think you are?

She takes my face in her hands. "I prayed you would be older when it happened." She glances at the cherub. "But when she arrived in your room that night, I knew it was my time."

269

"You knew about her?" I shout, suddenly furious again, shaking myself free. "We thought she was here for Raphael!" I look up at him standing awkwardly next to us. He looks horrified.

"I didn't know you thought that," she says.

"Well, what else would I think?" I hiss.

I stare at her. At her pale tear-stained face and her shaking hands. I can see how frightened she is.

"I have always loved you, Cassie, since the day you were born. I know you may find that hard to believe. And I know I didn't always show it. One day you will understand."

I take her hands, fighting back tears. Is this enough? Is what she says enough to take away all the years of hurt? But I see something in her eyes I have never seen before. Is it possible she does love me?

"It was my way of dealing with it. I thought if we weren't too close, it would be easier. When I left."

"I am your daughter," I say quietly. "Not your dog! Of course I'm going to become close to you!"

"I was thinking about me," she says. "I know that now. I never meant to hurt you, Cassie. You must believe me." She squeezes my hands. "Remember this. I will always be within you – within your soul. You are brave, braver than you think. Never forget that." She grips my arms so hard I cry out. "Know that I will be with you." She takes my hand and presses it against my chest. "With every beat of your heart, I will always be with you."

The fear and anger that have chipped at her features for as long as I can remember are softened by something I have never seen in her. Her eyes meet mine, and I feel her love wrap round me like a blanket. No one will ever take this feeling from me. Her heart, like mine, is broken. Bitter regrets nip at my insides – of time I can never get back – and as I look up at her, her eyes swimming with tears, I know she feels the same. I am consumed by her sadness and her fear of a future she did not want. A future she never chose.

I am overwhelmed by the sweet smell of almonds, the scent of a heavenly body, and weep.

She gently lets me go.

"Is it time?" I say, my voice trembling.

She nods.

Papa takes Mother in his arms. "My Queen of the Night," he whispers. "My rebellious bird."

"Goodbye, my love," she says, smiling at him, and he kisses her on her lips.

A bright light appears above us and the air is filled with the sweetest song – it is soft and lyrical, like a lullaby.

Bodies of light appear. They are the angels. Come for Mother.

"*You are not alone,*" they sing. "*On to eternity. Sing with me.*"

Wide bright eyes look down on us.

I take Mother's hand. She looks down at me and smiles. "Tremble not, dear daughter," she says.

"Can you ever come back?" I whisper.

"Perhaps one day, when you are old like me," she says. "But for now you must learn to live without me."

She turns to Raphael, kohl-stained tears now streaming down her face. "I am sorry you are like me," she says. "I know you didn't want this either, but be a better person than me."

Raphael nods and hangs his head.

The cherub, dishevelled and weak-looking, flies to me. I pull her into my arms and our hearts begin to beat as one. The feeling is so strong it takes my breath away. I press my cheek against hers, while she takes from me what she needs. "I've worked it out," I whisper. "It is love that nurtures you and makes you strong. I know that now."

I kiss her cheek. I can't be angry with her. Like Crunch and Grind, she was just doing what she had to do.

She dits and dahs in my ear.

My thanks.

My love.

The cherub looks at me through jet-black eyes and I feel a new connection between us. She has made me a promise. My grief at losing her is gone. Somehow I know I will see her again.

Mother beats her wings and rises above us, the cherub by her side to keep her safe on her long journey. As they rise through the roof, the angels come to them and envelop them in their song. It is a song of love and loss and longing. And of forgiveness too.

And then they are gone. I fall to my knees and weep.

Raphael sinks to his knees next to me. "I didn't know, Cassie!"

"I know," I say.

Papa joins us and wraps his arms round us both.

Crunch and Grind are quiet and stare at their feet. "We need to see to Emaline," they say. I nod as they leave, to thank them. And only when they are gone do I realise who they are. They are the Guardians. As old as the forest and the sky and the rock on which we stand, and, like the cherub, perhaps even as old as the Earth itself. Here forever to protect the poor wingless angels as they rise. Like my great-great-grandfather and his message that travelled through time. To protect us. To keep us safe.

I look up at the now empty night sky and quietly say goodbye to Mother and the cherub one last time.

Raphael takes my hand. It is just us now.

Raphael and Papa and me, with a secret we can never share. Knowing that one day the angels will come again.

Epilogue

It is a year since Mother was taken from us. The house is quiet without her, but we are adjusting to that now. Grandma died soon after Mother left. The pain of losing them both feels unbearable some days, but I'm keeping busy, and with every day that passes I feel a little stronger and more able to cope with the silence they left behind.

The grandfather clock announces it's eight o'clock. Papa, with Brutus by his side, is preparing a birthday feast for Frau Fischer consisting of Jägerschnitzel, a rabbit fricassee, Dampfnudel and potato salad. Lost in a sea of steam from the pans bubbling on the range, he chats as he stirs and sips, flinging in salt and herbs in wild flourishes. I chop mushrooms at the table. Freshly foraged this morning, they smell of the damp forest floor. Papa's telling me something about a lecture he's giving in München later this month, but I'm not listening.

I dreamed about Mother again last night, and I can't shake the memory from my mind. Frau Fischer, perhaps noticing my reverie, squeezes my knee and smiles at me. I catch her watching me sometimes, and little signs of affection are enough to bring a lump to my throat. I know she isn't my mother, but she's the closest I have to that now.

I often wonder what Mother would have been like if she hadn't had to keep me at a distance to protect her secret. Papa tried to explain it. About how Mother was complicated because of what she was.

And then we'd unearthed all her letters to Papa and me. Drawers stuffed full of the things. The half-finished attempts at an explanation. An occasional apology. How much she feared the owls because of what they might predict. Why she found it so difficult to be what we wanted her to be. How she could not bear to leave us.

How terrified she was.

Grandma told us just after Mother was taken that Mother, like Raphael, had also been left in the forest. A wingless angel, adopted by Grandma and Grandpa. As she grew up she proved to be a talented singer, yet was rebellious and headstrong. Grandma feared Mother might run away if she knew her fate, and because of that initially kept the truth hidden from her. Mother didn't grow wings at the usual age, and Grandma prayed that her daughter would not become a fully fledged angel. When Mother was eighteen, she joined the opera company in München and shortly afterwards married Papa. They returned home with me. But Grandma says that Mother, like Raphael, was plagued by dreams about a celestial world she didn't understand.

We always eat in the kitchen these days – Papa, Frau Fischer and me. The dining room is set up for lectures and exhibitions so isn't suitable for dining in any more. Papa is quite eminent now, renowned for his "discovery" of a pair of giant hawks with bones of glass. People pay a fortune to listen to his talks and witness with their own eyes the now infamous remains. *I* think he should have let them burn on Crunch and Grind's huge bonfire the day after everything happened, but Papa was insistent we should keep just two for posterity.

Frau Fischer came to live with us after being discharged from the sanatorium. She has brought new life to the house, and Papa and her often stay up into the early hours, talking over each other – about Mother, Raphael and, sometimes, me. He still cries about Mother, of course, but only when he thinks I'm not looking.

Olga now lives in Raphael's garden, and Frau Fischer often totters down our helter-skelter road to visit her and Raphael. She tells us the steep climb back up to our house is doing wonders for her legs.

There is a polite knock at the kitchen door. It is Raphael and his father. Frau Fischer squawks with excitement at the sight of Raphael.

"Oh, my boy," she cries, leaping up to greet him, wrapping her arms round his waist. Raphael's father greets her with a polite nod. He's apologised a hundred times for the way Raphael was taken from her all those years ago, and Frau Fischer seems to have forgiven him.

I help Raphael out of his long cloak and he sits down opposite me. His wings are now fully grown. They are quite beautiful – not white like Mother's – but a hundred shades of iridescent grey and brown. He tells me it is a huge relief when he can display them without fear of discovery. He has barely spoken about Mother's departure, knowing that one day the same will happen with him. I haven't been able to talk to him about it either. For now we simply admire his wings and try not to look too far into the future.

"Any sightings of those birds?" he says after they have settled at the table. Like the rest of us, he still worries about when they'll return.

We all shake our heads. We suspect the Sturmfalken travelled to Earth under the cover of a storm cloud soon after the cherub's arrival and hid in the castle until Strix was released and they were ready to attack, but, beyond that, we just don't know. We wonder if Emaline even summoned them herself, or whether they simply followed the cherub here. Papa thinks we will never know exactly what happened as Emaline refused to answer any of Crunch and Grind's questions.

Most of all we wish we knew why Emaline did what she did. Papa said, after discovering hundreds of tiny puncture marks in the eagle owl husk, that she must have rehydrated Strix by administering a substance through a syringe, slowly restoring him to life. The rat remains a mystery, but we suspect it was some sort of warning. Perhaps she was simply trying to frighten Mama; she clearly didn't like her very much. Crunch and Grind banished Emaline from Edenburg soon after everything happened and warned her never to return.

They called her the *anti-Guardian*, but refused to elaborate on exactly what that meant. They have assured me she won't come back, even when it's Raphael's time to rise, and I want to believe they're right. We're all a little embarrassed that none of us knew how long she'd been with us. Apparently she's as old as the Earth, like Crunch and Grind, and had been waiting quietly for the next angel rising.

"And how is Rufus the Rat?" Papa says to Raphael.

"He is most well behaved, thank you. No mystery demons or dark spirits lurking as far as I can tell."

"I'd burn it if it were my rat," Frau Fischer says brightly. "I wouldn't trust that rodent one inch!"

We all wish Raphael would get rid of the rat, but he seems attached to it.

"Oh, I forgot to mention, Crunch and Grind will be joining us for dinner," Papa says. "I bumped into them earlier. They seemed pleased to be asked."

Frau Fischer claps her hands together happily. "Ooh, I haven't seen those girls for a while. How wonderful!"

The doorbell rings. Of course no one moves.

"I'll go," I say eventually.

★

Crunch and Grind are used to the zip now and we travel up through the house in a comfortable silence. I notice, squashed between them, that they smell of coal tar soap. Crunch is wearing a new pair of lederhosen and Grind appears to be in some sort of skirt, although I'm not sure exactly what it is.

"How's your father?" Crunch asks as we rise.

"He's well, thank you," I reply.

"Still off the schnapps?"

I nod. He couldn't have managed the withdrawal symptoms without them. "He's making supper tonight!"

They both groan. "So long as it's better than last time," Grind says.

Crunch laughs. "Oh yes, let us hope so!" she says, slapping her thigh.

They'd admitted to me soon after the attack that Emaline hadn't summoned them that day, as I had suspected. They'd come because they knew that Mother was about to rise and wanted to protect Grandma from the shock of it all, as well as defending Mother from the Sturmfalken. When Grandma had fallen into a morphine-induced sleep, they had gone looking for Emaline, concerned, like me, about her intentions, and that is when they found her throttling me in the engine room. Of course they knew all about Raphael and had been keeping an eye on him for years, leaving a healing poultice at exactly the right time and

281

ensuring I discovered the pamphlet about what happens when an angel grows wings.

I think about the cherub every day, and still miss her, despite her visit being so brief. I know she needed me to love her to give her the strength to protect my mother, but from the moment I first held her in my arms, I truly did love her. It was the most natural thing in the world. And I think she loved me too.

Papa serves dinner at half past nine. The Jägerschnitzel is a little burnt at the edges and the potatoes quite gloopy-looking, but everyone makes polite "oohs" and "aahs" as I hand them their plates. It certainly smells delicious.

Frau Fischer tucks in almost before her plate has touched the table. "Oh, you're an angel," she says, beaming at Papa.

Bram weaves in and out of my legs, and then suddenly leaps up and hauls himself on to my lap with his claws. Wincing, I unhook him from my dress and wrap my arms round him. His body rattles with purrs.

"And how are you fine ladies?" Papa asks of Crunch and Grind when they have wiped their plates clean. I examine them discreetly. Are they really as old as the Earth? Raphael tells me that Guardians can live for ever, so no one knows exactly how old they are.

"Well, thank you," they say in unison.

And then Crunch mentions the thing that no one else has dared talk about, and my heart sinks.

"Cassie, we have a question for you."

The table falls silent and everyone turns to look at me.

"Have you had any dreams?" She hesitates. "Or any pain?"

My mother was an angel, and ever since that day I have been terrified that I might be part angel too.

"No." I shake my head. I hope that will be the end of the conversation.

Papa pushes his chair from the table and walks to the window. "There's a bright star up there tonight, Cassie," he says. "Might be worth a look. I opened the roof earlier, just in case…"

We search the sky most nights for a sign of Mother. Something to tell us she is not gone forever. That she is watching over us.

★

Raphael and I climb on to the zip platform together, and I reach for the lever to start generating some steam, but he gently pulls my hand away.

"What are you doing?" I say. "Would you rather take the stairs?"

"No, it's not that," he says. "I just thought that maybe we don't need to use the zip tonight."

His wings are outstretched.

My heart misses a beat.

He takes my hands in his.

"What are you doing?" I whisper.

"Do you trust me?"

"Of course," I say.

He beats his wings.

Our feet lift up from the platform.

Together we rise, passing through each hole cut by Grandpa a lifetime ago, breathing in the sights and smells of my strange house. Raphael's eyes are fixed on mine. He's smiling slightly, giving me the courage I need to rise with him, taking away my fear. And so we rise in silence, feeling lighter than the air. And in this stillness it feels for the briefest moment that our hearts are beating as one.

Acknowledgements

Eternal thanks to everyone at Nosy Crow, especially Kirsty Stansfield for taking *Fledgling* under your wing and for helping to make it the best it could be, and to Fi Scoble too. To David Dean for the divine cover art, and to Nicola Theobald for turning it into this beautiful book.

To Joanna Moult for being my perfect agent, for believing in *Fledgling* and for finding it the best home at Nosy Crow.

To the staff on the MA in Writing for Young People at Bath Spa. To Janine Amos for your kindness and guidance, to David Almond for writing *Skellig*, my inspiration for *Fledgling*, to Julia Green for your wisdom, and Lucy Christopher for being an inspiration!

To my fabulous MA friends – Anna Crowe, Sarah Stevens, Anne Manson, Andrea Fowkes, Carly Squires, Lis Jardine, Kate Mallinder and Anna Clothier, thank you for your support and friendship.

To Team Skylark, for welcoming me into the nest; I dedicate Olga the goat to you all! To The Good Ship 2021 and the Southbank Writers.

To Becky Quew-Jones for telling me for thirty years to write a book. I'm glad I finally listened to you. To my

Bristol chums, for everything. To those who bravely read my first attempt at a book (you know who you are!) but with special thanks to Tessa and Eloise for your most excellent feedback.

To my ancestors! The lives you lived inspired many of the characters in this story. To my grandfather, who, like Cassie's Papa, was broken by war. To my brave great-uncles killed in the Second World War. To my great-grandfather who wrote our family history, leaving behind his voice for future generations. How I wish he'd left me a message on a gramophone player! And to my magnificent great-uncle, Andrew Campbell, who, in the 1960s, blasted a road up to his Welsh mountaintop house with dynamite (in the days when you were allowed to do such things), inspiring Cassie's helter-skelter road.

To my mum, who I'm happy to say is nothing like Cassie's mother! Thank you, Mum, for everything; for bringing me into the world, for all those trips to the library, and for always being so supportive about my writing!

To my wonderful children, Hattie and Dylan. Above all else, to Kev, for always believing in me, for your brilliant feedback and plot ideas, and for being by my side through my moments of self-doubt. I couldn't have done this without you!